IT IS AN
HONEST
GHOST
JOHN
GOLDBACH

Coach House Books | Toronto

first edition

 Canada Council **Conseil des Arts**
for the Arts du Canada

 ONTARIO ARTS COUNCIL
CONSEIL DES ARTS DE L'ONTARIO
an Ontario government agency
un organisme du gouvernement de l'Ontario

Canadä

Published with the generous assistance of the Canada Council for the
Arts and the Ontario Arts Council. Coach House Books also acknowledges
the support of the Government of Canada through the Canada Book
Fund and the Government of Ontario through the Ontario Book Publish-
ing Tax Credit.

LIBRARY AND ARCHIVES CANADA CATALOGUING IN PUBLICATION

Goldbach, John, 1978-, author
    It is an honest ghost / John Goldbach. -- First edition.

Short stories.
Issued in print and electronic formats.
ISBN 978-1-55245-333-9 (paperback)

    I. Title.

PS8613.O432I85 2016   C813'.6   C2015-908208-0

It Is an Honest Ghost is available as an ebook: ISBN 978-1-77056-451-0
(EPUB), ISBN 978-1-77056-452-7 (PDF), ISBN 978-1-77056-461-9 (MOBI).

Purchase of the print version of this book entitles you to a free digital
copy. To claim your ebook of this title, please email sales@chbooks.com
with proof of purchase or visit chbooks.com/digital. (Coach House Books
reserves the right to terminate the free digital download offer at any time.)

To Madeleine

'Maybe a man's name doesn't matter all that much.'
— Orson Welles, from *F for Fake*

CONTENTS

AN OLD STORY:
IN FIVE PARTS

I

An old story: disappointments in love, debts unpaid, a series of lousy apartments, a series of lousy jobs, betrayals, some rancour, some sickness, etc. He in many ways was typical but it was in fact the amassing of these specific typical experiences that made him an individual, he liked to think. After a long winter, with its blizzards and periodic power outages and frozen pipes and eternal darkness, spring had arrived, with its budding branches and populated streets and clear blue skies and women in skirts. Something like hope. By mid-May, after weeks of drinking in bars again and trying to meet new women, he once again fell into his solitary winter ways. The promise of the new was not dead and buried, though it once again felt distant, he decided, one mild afternoon, sitting at his kitchen table. The days passed and each day he'd go through his routine, or one of the four or five routines he'd formed and mixed up, in a sense, to keep from confronting the fact that he was a creature of habit, and perhaps temperament, who had much in common with a marmot. Still, even with his varied routines, he thought about a certain inescapable mundanity that he feared came from within but hated to confront so he rarely did, that is to say, confront it.

II

Instead, he altered and augmented his already-existing routines, taking new streets when he walked to work, stopping in stores he'd never been in before, even going into bookstores that sold books in languages he couldn't read. He read in parks. One night, around dusk, when people walk their dogs while the sun sets, he sat on a park bench, by a pond, reading in the last light. He continued reading and his mind wandered, but he reread the words and sentences and paragraphs he'd passed over, lost in thoughts that had little to do with the book in his hands. A woman with a child and dog walked past the bench. He imagined they quickened their pace when they approached the bench. The sky was more blue than orange. The geese were dark in the sky, flying in awkward formation. He watched them disappear into the dark blue. The park lights gradually came on, humming gently; he stood up and walked away when they came to full light.

III

At night he'd read on his couch for hours on end and often until daybreak, or until he fell asleep, whichever came first. Sometimes he drank. When he drank, however, he'd still read, though absently – that is to say, more absently than usual. While absently reading, he'd often dream of past loves, though not necessarily of past events. He'd dream of new and impossible events, with a strong sense of the past running through these fantasies for the sake of verisimilitude. The nights were long, not surprisingly, though he nevertheless occupied them, with varying degrees of success. First thing every morning, he'd put the kettle on the burner and make mug after mug of steaming Gunpowder Green Tea. Again, he'd submit to routine. Love might be infinite, he'd think, though we're cracked under its impossible pressures.

IV

Mid-summer it rained for days, a tireless downpour. He avoided going outside. A cat screeched and yowled in the rain on the fire escape outside his window, though he did nothing. It isn't my cat, he thought. The days looked like nights and the nights went on and on. He was finding it difficult to concentrate. He was finding it difficult to sleep. Nothing seemed to maintain his interest, though he submitted to his routines nonetheless. He'd diagnosed his life as hollow and senseless, and the world followed suit. Cars hydroplaned in the rain and sounded like ocean waves. Thunder rumbled continuously. While sitting at his kitchen table, he thought, I've slipped through the grates of a storm sewer. The cat screeched and yowled above the waves.

V

He sat on a park bench. The sun set. Shadows of leaves shuddered quickly on the pale asphalt path. It would be an hour or so until night. He held a book in his hands, though he wasn't following what he was reading; instead, he was thinking about a woman sitting on a red blanket and reading across the pond on the grassy embankment. He wondered how he could possibly talk to her. He wondered what he'd possibly say. It seemed so impossible, walking over to her, introducing himself, starting up conversation. The water on the surface of the pond rippled in the breeze. He considered removing his wristwatch, then asking her if she had the time. That's stupid, he thought. He read absently as the sun set and across the pond a beautiful woman read, too. The sky darkened while the park lights slowly warmed. He closed his book and looked across the pond, where not minutes ago the beautiful woman had been reading, though now she was gone and he sat still on the bench. He waited until the lights reached full intensity, then he stood to walk home.

IT IS AN HONEST GHOST

The night wind blew loudly and we sat in the car in the mill parking lot talking, watching the tree boughs bend and sway to and fro and almost break. Soon, I thought, a branch on one of these evergreens will snap in the blustering wind and fly around aimlessly. We were waiting for James. He'd run into the mill to cash a paycheque for Allan from one of the tills in the old safe in the office. It was Allan's McDonald's paycheque; he had signed the back, and we sat waiting in James's 1974 Buick Riviera. We were going drinking downtown. A band we liked was playing; we had just dropped acid.

James returned and got in behind the wheel and counted out six twenties and passed them to Allan, saying, 'Here you go, fucker.'

'Thanks,' said Allan, pocketing the bills. 'Let's drink!'

'Hear, hear,' I said.

And James spun out the back tires and whipped the car around and sped up the mill hill. The acid hadn't kicked in yet, or not really, but every once in a while we'd ask each other if it had taken effect. Slowly, it did. We all smoked and music played loudly; James had installed a stolen CD player where the old dial radio used to be. He'd installed some stolen speakers, too, that he'd bought from the back of a truck at a gas station. They sounded like shit.

James wasn't drinking but he'd nevertheless taken acid, though it hadn't really kicked in yet. He claimed he drove fine on acid. The streetlights passed by quickly as we descended into the city and the fields turned to strip malls and fast food and gas stations and apartment buildings, all with large parking lots. We kept on driving straight toward downtown, winding with the street, with no other traffic around. There was plenty of parking behind the club. James parked far from other cars; the lot was mainly dark save some lights by the booth, where no attendant sat.

'I don't think we have to pay,' said Allan. 'Or at least no one's there.'

'Fuck it,' said James and cut the engine, and we all got out.

There was a line out front winding around the corner, but Allan told us just to follow him, and we did, and when we got to the door they let us in, stamped our hands, patted our backs while pushing us forward, and we made our way toward one of the bars. It was loud already and some band was playing, though none of us knew their name and no one we asked at the bar seemed to have any idea who they were, either. But they were loud and the vocals were distorted and so was the guitar and bass and the drums were heavy, too, and fast. Allan and I got beers and James got a Coke. We went outside to the patio with our drinks.

'The band sounds like shit,' said James.

'I'd have to agree with you,' said Allan, an unlit cigarette in his mouth.

'I'm feeling it,' I said. 'The acid, not the band.'

'Me too,' said Allan.

And James nodded, though he looked a little scared. But we said nothing and smoked. The moon was bright and there were rippling cloudbanks that moved fast past the moon, screening it briefly but sheer.

'When do they go on?' said James.

'Next,' said Allan. 'I'm feeling it. I'm definitely feeling it.'

James and I nodded, our bloodshot eyes wide open.

We went inside and the music was loud, the band was screaming, it seemed like all of them were screaming, and it was all distorted and muddy and we moved into the crowd toward the stage but quickly turned around as the crowd pushed and slammed into each other the closer we got to the stage. We moved back toward the bar.

'I kind of want to get the fuck out of here,' I said.

'I wouldn't mind leaving, either,' said James.

'Sure,' said Allan. 'I don't really care.'

'Let's head back to the mill,' I said.

As we left the bar, there was still a line bending around the corner. The car was as we had left it and there wasn't a ticket on the windshield. We piled in and spun out of the parking lot and northward toward the mill. The streetlights cast large shadows of their poles, stretching out like elastic arms, like the guy from the Fantastic Four, the leader, though I'd forgotten his name – Dr. Something, I thought.

No one was talking and we were left alone with our bending thoughts. Eventually, Allan broke the silence.

'I need something salty,' he said. 'Can we get some nuts or something from the mill?'

'Sure,' said James.

The Riviera descended the dark mill hill and in its lights were geese waddling out of the way, some hissing, wings spread, waddling quickly, and we pulled into the mill parking lot.

'What the fuck?' said James, stopping the car.

'What?' we said.

'The office light,' he said, motioning with his head, hands gripping the wheel. 'It's always left on. It's how my dad says we can tell if someone came in and tried to rob the safe.'

'How's that?' said Allan.

'Chances are they'll think they turned on the light and shut it off on their way out.'

'Are you saying you think someone tried to rob the safe while we were gone?' I said. 'You probably shut the light off after you went in and cashed Al's cheque.'

'Of course that's what happened,' said Allan. 'Come on. It's not like someone's been here and robbed the mill in the hour we've been gone.'

'You never know,' said James. 'And I know I didn't shut that light off. We always leave it on – when I was a little kid, even, I'd be lectured on never shutting off the light. It's ingrained in me to never shut off the office light. My grandfather never shut it off. My dad never shuts it off. I never shut it off. Everybody knows not to shut it off.'

'Maybe a bulb burnt out,' I said.

'There're a couple of fluorescent lights.'

'Man, you were rushing in to cash my cheque,' said Allan. 'You probably just shut it off. I mean, we're on acid.'

'Yeah, but we'd just taken it.'

'Maybe the power went out,' I offered.

Pointing toward the mill's third-floor windows, James said, 'Then why are those lights on?'

'Man, I just highly doubt someone robbed the place. Could be a blown fuse.'

'Let's go in and check,' said Allan.

We got out of the car and the moon was still above us, above the valley, over the highway, and the cloud cover was still moving quickly past the moon. The branches were blowing around and leaves were blowing from the walls of the valley and around the parking lot.

'Are you freaked out?' said Allan to James, who answered, 'A little.'

'I'm sure it's nothing,' I said.

We walked up the ramp to the loading dock in single file – James, Allan and me – and stopped at the large door as James inserted a small key in the large padlock and the lock popped and he slid it off the staple and opened the hasp and hooked the lock back on the ring, saying, 'I've got a really bad feeling about this,' and he looked greenish and worried. 'I'm not sure I want to do this.'

'So why don't we call your dad,' I said, 'or the police.'

'Are you out of your mind,' said Allan. 'The police! I don't know about you but I'm on acid and the idea of talking to the police right now is nuts.'

'You're right, you're right,' I said. 'I didn't mean it.'

'Let's just check it out,' said Allan.

James looked at us and opened the door, pressing his shoulder up against it, pushing with his whole body as we gathered behind him. The door opened widely on to the dark mill and James made his way directly past the machinery and quickly into the store, where the office was, and Allan and I followed. The store was dark and James moved past the shelves of various types of flour and nuts and bird-seeds, etc., and toward the office and turned on the light and said, '*Ha!*' and we jumped. But when I looked, there was no one in the office and the safe was closed and presumably locked.

'No one's been here,' I said. 'Or at least no one has tampered with the safe.'

'It doesn't appear that way,' said James, while assuring the safe was locked.

'Well, mystery solved,' said Allan.

'What do you mean? We still don't know who turned off the light.'

'You did,' said Allan.

'No,' said James. 'I didn't.'

'Then it was a ghost.'

'The switch was turned off. Why would a ghost do that?'

'How am I supposed to know what an apparition would do,' said Allan. 'I don't know any ghosts.'

'They terrorize,' I said.

'How terrifying,' said Allan. 'They turned off the lights.'

'I didn't say it was a ghost,' said James. 'You said it was a ghost.'

'I said it was you. And if not you, then a ghost.'

'Well, it wasn't me.'

'I'd say it could've been somebody else but there are no signs of forced entry,' I said.

'Does it matter?' said Allan. 'Everything's okay,' he added. 'Nothing's been tampered with and nothing's been stolen and everyone's okay and maybe James's arm brushed the switch on the way out. Who knows. It doesn't matter now.'

As soon as Allan finished, the lights went out and some-body jumped and it felt like the room jumped.

'What the fuck is that?' said James.

'It's okay, man,' I said, 'the power's gone out. It'll come back on.'

And it did. Immediately.

'That did freak me out,' said Allan.

'Me too,' I said. 'But it's just the weather. The wind's really picking up. Listen to it.'

And everyone went silent. And the high-pitched wind whistled fiercely, without pause.

'This is creepy,' said Allan. 'But I'm sure it's nothing; we're all just high.'

'Yeah,' we said.

'Everything's okay,' I said, 'so there's nothing to worry about. We should lock up the mill and go back to the house.'

'Okay,' said James. But then we heard the sound of breaking glass, a window shattering, I thought, and it was clear James and Allan had the same thought.

'That came from upstairs,' said James. 'I think the second floor.'

'NOT IT,' I said.

'NOT IT,' said Allan.

'I'm not going up alone. You guys are coming with,' said James.

We followed, again in single file, as James led the way with a flashlight, though the lights were on, too. We went back into the mill proper – by the first, second and third breaks, the sifters, etc. – and up the first flight of dusty wooden stairs. The mill smelled of the diesel fuel that was used to mop up the wooden floors. The stairs creaked, the mill creaked, bending, as the loud wind bent everything.

'It's a branch,' said James, pointing the flashlight's beam at a broken bough that had smashed through one of the second-floor windows; it lay atop shards of glass. You could feel the cold wind blowing in the shattered window from the top of the stairs.

'Wow,' said Allan. 'That's some wind.' He noticeably shivered.

'What should we do?' I said.

'Nothing,' said James. 'For right now. I'll clean it up later.'

'Well, at least we know it wasn't a ghost,' said Allan. 'Just a powerful wind.'

We scrambled down the stairs and back past the breaks and the sifters and the packer and the sewing machines suspended from the ceiling by a system of ropes and pulleys, where the flour bags would be packed and sewn shut. We went back in the store and into the office. James sat down at the dusty rolltop desk, with metal clips and papers all over it, small notebooks, pens, pencils, more clips and a few postcards, too. Old photos of the mill and damsite – some black-and-white and some grainy colour – and a few old photos of the millers and employees over the past seventy-odd years of the mill's two-hundred-year existence. James opened the bottom drawer of the rolltop desk and produced a bottle of whisky, with a note written on masking tape taped to it, and he read: 'DRINK IN CASE OF EMERGENCY.'

He stared at it and added, 'This qualifies,' and unscrewed the cap – the seal was already broken – and he took a deep swig, then passed it to Allan. After taking a swig, Allan passed it to me and I sipped lightly, then passed it back to James.

'Man,' said Allan, 'don't worry about who shut off the light. It was either you or some freak thing, you know. But it was probably you. Big deal.'

'It wasn't. I know it sounds weird, but I know it wasn't me.'

'Maybe someone else's been here,' I offered, 'like your dad, for example.'

'He's away,' said James. 'He's with his buddies in New York for the weekend.'

A crash was heard, from we weren't sure where, and we all jumped.

'I think that came from outside,' said James. 'It sounded like it came from the dock.'

And he stood up and left the office and walked toward the loading dock; we followed.

'It's just a cart,' he said, leaning over the dock, looking down at the parking lot, looking at a handcart lying on its side on the gravel and asphalt. 'It should be inside, anyway,' he added. 'I don't know what it's doing out here.'

James jumped off the dock and picked up the handcart and righted it and walked it over to the ramp and rolled it up to the dock, leaning in the wind as he walked. 'You know what?' he said. And then paused.

'What?' said Allan. 'We're on tenterhooks.'

'No,' he said. 'It's of no consequence.'

'What?' we said.

'People have died in this mill, you know, like worksite accidents.'

'So?' said Allan. 'So we're back to the poltergeist hypothesis? Are you saying it's more likely that the ghost of a dead miller shut off the lights than you? Because if you are,' he said, shaking his head, 'that's a little much.'

'First off, I'm not saying it was a ghost of a dead miller, for god's sake. Secondly, there have been ghost stories surrounding the mill, of course.'

'Why *of course*?' said Allan, scratching at his head.

'Well, you know,' said James, 'it's a two-hundred-year-old flour mill. It's an old building and kind of scary at night and people have died in the building, is all I'm saying, which means it isn't surprising that some ghost stories surround the place.'

'Like what?' said Allan. 'The Ghost of Christmas Past floats through here from time to time? Or maybe Casper?'

'Forget it.'

'No, no,' said Allan. 'Tell us your ghoulish tales.'

'All right,' said James. 'Get bent.'

'If you have a ghost story,' I said, 'I want to hear it.'

The wind was louder than the falls out back, but the falls could still be heard distantly, buried beneath the wind.

'No, it's just this one guy,' said James, looking at us wearily, 'named Matthew Higgins died in the mill around 1952, got caught in a belt and it snapped his neck, a piece of clothing or something, and after he died some strange stuff started happening, I heard.'

'Like what?' said Allan.

'Like just equipment started acting up all the time,' he said, 'and there were power outages all the time – and the millers would hear footsteps.'

'What's so strange about that?' I said.

'When no one else was around. When they were milling alone. When they were milling at night. There'd be reports that they'd heard footsteps. Even now, today, like sometimes Tadek says he hears footsteps at night when he's milling alone.'

'Man,' said Allan, 'the mill makes quite the racket when it's going – of course Tadek hears shit. It's an audio illusion or something, you know. What he perceives he hears he doesn't really hear. It's just a bunch of banging that sounds like footsteps.'

'Yeah,' said James, 'but sometimes his tools have been moved. Sometimes he says he knows, like knows for a fact, that he didn't leave some tool where he finds it.'

'Does he ever drink on the job?' I said.

'He doesn't really drink at all.'

'Maybe he just forgot that he'd moved whatever tools,' said Allan.

'I don't think so. He's got his routines.'

'You know ghosts aren't real?' said Allan. 'You know that, right, James? Like, once you're dead you're dead and you don't communicate with this world because you don't exist, like your ego and shit, it doesn't exist at all, so how would you go about haunting your old job site?'

'I'm not saying I believe in ghosts,' said James, 'but I do believe there are mysterious things that go on in this world and the universe that we can't explain.'

'Well, when you put it like that, yeah of course,' said Allan. 'But that doesn't mean that the ghost of some Higgins guy's floating around the mill moving Tadek's tools.'

'I'm not saying it's Matthew Higgins.'

'Or some other ghost.'

'I'm not saying it's a ghost.'

'You kind of are,' said Allan.

'I'm not. What's a ghost, anyway?' said James.

'I'm not following,' said Allan.

'Records are ghosts, for example, and books and movies,' said James.

'Books and movies and LPS are all just records – inanimate objects,' said Allan. 'We're the goddamn ghosts!'

'Haunting the planet temporarily,' said James.

'Something like that,' said Allan. 'Haunting each other at least.'

It wasn't raining, though I imagined it pouring, the mill pond flooding the banks.

'Okay,' I said. 'Let's just agree that it wasn't the ghost of Matthew Higgins that shut off the office lights and not worry about it because there's nothing to worry about, you know.'

'Agreed,' said Allan.

'Yeah,' said James. 'All right.'

'Don't be mad,' said Allan. 'We just don't believe in ghosts like you do.'

'I don't believe in ghosts. Well, but I don't not believe in them, either. It's not a matter of belief. You have brushes with them or you don't.'

'That's the dumbest thing I've ever heard,' said Allan.

'Why?'

'Why do you think?' he said. 'You're acting like only the elect get contact with the spirit world – and the rest of us go on living with the illusion that we're the only, like, sentient beings on the globe of our type, the human type, or with human-type intelligence, but you know, they're not alive ... '

'What?' said James.

'I'm one of the dumb ones,' said Allan, 'one of those assholes who doesn't believe in ghosts because I'm not special enough to commune with them. But then again I don't try enough, maybe. Where's your Ouija board, James? Time for some necromancy.'

'Man, I don't believe in free-floating spirits. I do, however, believe that sometimes the spirit of one person inhabits the body of another person, like after death, of course.'

'Of course,' said Allan.

I lit a cigarette and snapped the match toward the ground from the dock but it went out and took off in the wind.

'If after you die you come back as a ghost, I want to die,' said Allan.

'Psssst,' I said. 'Don't worry, you'll be dead soon enough.'

'But what's so crazy about that?' said James.

'Transmigration of souls,' said Allan.

'Yes, I think,' said James.

'You're having metempsychotic fantasies, James,' said Allan. 'Traits are passed on, obviously, through genetics and so on, but not actual souls. This idea of a soul is a byproduct of consciousness.'

'I don't follow,' said James. 'Didn't realize you've been eating dictionaries for dinner. But I do believe that people are reincarnated, so to speak.'

'No,' said Allan.

'How do you know?' I said.

'Because,' said Allan. 'Everything's probably happening at once, or in a blip, anyway,' he said, 'so how could souls, then, keep coming back, over and over again, when the entirety of human existence has happened in a flash already? History repeats itself but we don't!'

'Whoa, what?' said James.

'I think I sort of followed,' I said, inhaling smoke, thinking, though not very clearly, looking up at the sky, at the moon and the clouds.

'But you don't believe in ghosts?' said James.

'Neither do you, you said,' I said.

'I don't,' he said.

'You do,' said Allan.

'I want to know what Al means when he says that it's all already happened, like humanity,' said James.

'I don't know,' said Allan. 'It's sort of like we know it but can't admit it till it unfolds, as it unfolds. It's all already happened – Nero, Napoleon, now us – it's a lightning flash, never to return.'

'Well, that's quite interesting,' said James. 'Still, you don't believe in spooks.'

'So it's all happened already but it's all happening, too, and it's disappearing,' I said.

'I guess,' said Allan. 'It's a trace that's fading out.'

'So Fate's sealed?' I said.

'In a sense yes and in a sense no,' said Allan. 'It's going to go down but you have to play your part.'

'So that's my agency,' I said.

'I guess,' said Allan, lighting a cigarette. He started coughing as soon as he took the first drag, then said, 'A ghost's your future. And your present, too, I guess, in the sense that there's a *present*. And your past's certainly a ghost there below, obviously. You're your own ghost, always and forever.'

'Till you're not,' I said.

'Well, you're still a ghost – just one of a more etheric variety, a collection of egoless molecules amongst and now indecipherable from other molecules in, like, the great white ocean of oblivion.'

'Why white?' I said.

'I don't know – black or white,' said Allan. 'It's just the way I picture it. But there's a lot of muck on the road to there.' He was worked up and his voice was hoarse and he peered through the window into the mill and it looked like a puff of his breath hit the windowpane, briefly clouding it with hoarfrost, though as quickly as the icy cobwebs formed their complex crystalline patterns, they receded and vanished. 'It's freezing,' he said, shivering. 'Let's go inside.'

We went in the office and sat in chairs and sipped some more whisky, while talking more about ghosts and other things.

'Ghosts are an invention of man,' said Allan.

'Okay, okay,' said James. 'I don't believe in ghosts.'

'So who turned out the light?' said Allan.

'I sincerely don't know,' said James.

'That's a good answer,' I said. 'Time to leave him alone, Al. You bully people.'

'I bully people!' he said incredulously, sneering, adding, 'That's outrageous.'

'Yeah,' I said. 'Outrageous.'

'All I was saying, before you rudely interrupted me – '

'I didn't interrupt you.'

' – was that ghosts are a creation of man, like God is a creation of man – and/or gods, plural. Man's become a slave to his inventions before, you know – look at humankind's relationship to God, obviously, for example. And we'll become slaves to our computers, too – it's already happening, right? Anyway, James is a slave to the idea of apparitions, I think, who turn off office lights.'

'Okay, man, enough,' said James. 'I must've shut off the light. Are you happy now?'

'Yes,' said Allan.

'Good.'

'I've been happy all along,' he said.

The conversation eventually lulled and we dozed off from time to time. I couldn't really sleep well in the chair and I kept coming to and looking out the office window and then fading off again. Toward dawn, the mill parking lot filled with fog and the Riviera couldn't be made out, though the odd goose would pierce through the fog, craning its neck, hissing in the fog, all neck like a screaming white serpent save the tips of its wings, the tips of its spread wings that could be made out vaguely – a screaming winged serpent submerged in fuming smoke, scorched white.

STANDING IN FRONT OF
THE KAZAN CATHEDRAL:
ST. PETERSBURG,
RUSSIA, 2005

Tears began to form in his eyes while, thinking of his mother and brothers and father and sisters and friends and girlfriend, as he stood in front of the Kazan Cathedral, staring at its gold cross penetrating the blue sky, an artificial-looking sky, like a Technicolor movie sky, and the gold twinkling in the omnipresent sun, he dreamed of a video camera recording him, men in masks and a knife to his throat, all of these things he thought of while tears formed and he thought about what he'd say, what he'd do, in the last few minutes before these men, these men he had nothing to do with, decided to chop off his head, like they'd done to others, while staring at the spire shining in the bright sun, and tears were growing larger and starting to leak out of the corners of his eyes, but he'd be brave, he decided, not begging but smiling, smiling into the camera, and he'd say that he loved his mother and his brothers and his father and his sisters and his friends and girlfriend very much, especially his girlfriend, who was his favourite person that he'd ever met while living, and that he was grateful to her, perhaps, but that would sound lame so maybe he'd just tell everyone that he loved them all, keep it simple, not waste words, and be brave right before the men with the black balaclavas cut off his head and it fell to the dusty ground of some cave, though maybe he'd say something about his captors, too, like they were just fools so the world should forgive them, something Christlike and understanding, something full of infinite love, since he wouldn't have to make good on that love but rather he'd just die and be done with it so he could afford to say something special and sweet for the world to remember his boundless benevolence by and he hoped that people would miss him, miss him so much, and he thought about Tom Sawyer and going to one's own funeral and he wondered what people would say, if they'd express anger over his terrorist kidnappers or if they'd talk about what could've been, the potential he wouldn't have to make good on but would nevertheless be remembered for because he'd had his head chopped off by terrorists in some remote locale, as a result of some conflict he had nothing to do with, and the clouds moved fast past the Kazan Cathedral in the big blue northern sky, and he started to cry a little more as he pictured his brothers hugging his mother, his girlfriend sedated with pills, everyone dressed in black, and his father silent as stone as his friends smoked cigarettes, not knowing what to say to one another, simply shaking their heads in disbelief, and he started shaking, thinking of all the people he loved mourning him and missing him and they wouldn't be able to forget about him because he was killed by terrorists so he'd have scholarships named after him and maybe a day named after him, too, or a street or something, or a statue like Field Marshal Kutuzov, in his hometown and then he said, *This is ridiculous and narcissistic*, and his thoughts started to calm down.

A GIRL WITH A
DRAGON TATTOO

'**M**ark Phillips.'
    'What? Sorry?'
'Mark Phillips.'
'How do you know my name?'
'You don't remember me.'
'I'm sorry, no I don't.'
'Think.'
'I am.'
'Think harder.'
'Yeah. Well, I'm thinking hard.'
'Right. Think hard.'
'Give me a clue.'
'This is too fun.'
'Nothing?'
'Come with me.'
'I don't know.'
'You're safe.'
'I hope so.'
'Come.'

'This is slightly awkward.'
    'What?'
    'Well, you know, you know my name and I don't know yours and ... '

'And ... '

'Well ... '

'Just relax and enjoy.'

'Don't get me wrong, I'm enjoying this.'

'Me too.'

'But seriously, how do you know my name?'

'Do you think I'm hot?'

'Yes, extremely, of course. And that's some tattoo.'

'You like it?'

'I do. It's long.'

'I know – it goes all the way from the top of my right butt cheek to the tip of my left shoulder blade.'

'I can see that.'

'And you like it?'

'I do.'

'It's hot, right?'

'Very.'

'I like you.'

'Thanks. I like you too.'

'I've always thought you were nice and cute.'

'Thanks, but *always*? Seriously, how do you know me?'

'You have no idea.'

'I don't. I really don't.'

'You want a clue?'

'Yes – please!'

'All right. But this might make it too obvious ... '

'Okay.'

'We went to high school together.'

'Sunnyside?'

'Yep.'

'Wow! Really? You went to Sunnyside ... What year?'

'Same as you.'

'No way.'

'Way.'

'How come I can't place you?'

'I look different.'

'You look amazing.'

'I look a lot different.'

'So you weren't a blond.'

'No, I wasn't. But my hair was dyed then, too.'

'What colour?'

'Black. Jet black.'

'So you had jet-black hair and we were in the same year.'

'Yes.'

'Were you sort of a goth?'

'Yes. I wore black twenty-eye Doc Martens and torn fishnets.'

'Anything else?'

'We used to smoke in the pit together sometimes.'

'When?'

'After Grade 10 math.'

'Erin Blake!'

'You got it!'

'Holy shit.'

'I've lost a lot of weight.'

'I can't believe it … '

'I know. Sorry for playing with you – I couldn't resist.'

'It's okay. Wow.'

'Don't feel weird.'

'No, just … How long have you been dancing?'

'A year or so.'

'Do you like it?'

'I love it.'

'Why?'

'Well, first off, I make about $2,500 a week and I only work three or four shifts.'

'That's great. Wow. Erin Blake.'

'Yeah. By the way, though, my name here's Pamela.'

'Right. What else do you like about it?'

'I like the power I have over men now. I feel like I understand them better. I feel like I can get them to do almost anything.'

'Does it ever get creepy?'

'Oh yeah, of course.'

'Like how, for instance?'

'Like a couple of weeks ago I was dancing with my back turned to this guy, bending over, and I looked between my legs while holding my ankles, and he had his cock in his hand and was beating off, like really aggressively, and that was fucked up.'

'What did you do?'

'I called for Jerry, one of the bouncers, and he was in here in a second and dragged him out into the street with his dick in his hand and kicked the shit out of him.'

'Holy shit!'

'Yeah.'

'That's fucked up.'

'Yeah. But most of the time guys are respectful and know that the bouncers will kill them if they fuck with the girls.'

'That makes sense.'

'Men are really simple, or at least they are when they come in here. They want to drink and they want to see naked women.'

'Right.'

'I mean, a lot of guys will ask me what I'm doing later, like after my shift, but I don't date guys I meet here and I'm not a whore.'

'So you have guys offer you money for sex?'

'All the time. Some old guy once offered me a thousand bucks to give him a hand job in his BMW.'

'What did you say?'

'Hey!'

'Ouch!'

'Did that actually hurt?'

'No, not really.'

'Okay, good. But I can't believe you'd ask that – of course I said no!'

'Well, sorry, but I haven't seen you in, like, eight years and you used to be a goth and you wore twenty-eye Docs and now you're blond and wearing stilettos and a G-string, you know, and you've got this very large dragon tattoo ... So I don't know what you'd say ... '

'I'm not a whore.'

'I never said you were!'

'I know but I'm not. So you know. Never.'

'Okay, cool. Good.'

' ... '

'How did you know it was a BMW?'

'What?'

'His car.'

'He told me. This isn't a bordello. I'm sure some of the girls make a little extra money on the side, but I'm not one of them.'

'What were you doing before dancing, after high school?'

'Well, you probably don't remember, but I left Sunnyside in Grade 11 – basically dropped out – because I was bullied so much, so I got the fuck out of that shit hole.'

'You were bullied?'

'Mercilessly.'

'Why?'

'It's a long story, kind of ... But do you remember Heather Waller?'

'Well, yes, sort of ... You mean the girl who died of a brain tumour?'

'Yes, her.'

'She died the year I got to high school. I remember because there was an assembly in memoriam of her but I'd never met her but nevertheless there seemed something holy about her to me, you know, because she died so young and people were so upset, of course.'

'I was best friends with Alex Waller, her younger sister, in middle school. I was friends with Heather, too. And when she got really sick, when she had no hair anymore and everyone was pretty much certain she was going to die, I was at a friend's house in Thorndale, not far from the Wallers', and Alex was there and one of the girls didn't like me – this bitch, Julie Pitt – '

'I remember her ... '

'Well, she's a fucking cunt ... Anyway, Julie told Alex and the other girls that I'd been making fun of Heather's hair loss. She said I was making fun of Heather for being bald. Heather was my friend and Alex was my best friend and Julie told this awful lie about me and for some reason everyone believed her – I still don't know why. I told Alex it was a lie – I told everyone it was a lie – but no one believed me, and a couple of weeks later Heather was dead. And you're right, then high school started and this vicious, just plain stupid lie followed me there and made my life a living hell.'

'I had no idea. Really? That's a terrible story. Were you in touch with Alex again?'

'Not really. I tried, and then she moved to Sarnia with her family, who were devastated, and it seemed like there was no point, in a way, after a while.'

'So, who bullied you?'

'Everybody, pretty much.'

'I didn't know, really, like at all.'

'I know. That's one of the reasons I liked you. We talked in math class a bit and we'd smoke out in the pit and you were nice and always stoned and totally oblivious to my rep as someone who makes fun of friends dying of cancer.'

'Yeah, that's certainly not how I thought of you. So what happened when you left high school?'

'I moved to the States, lived in Detroit briefly, after staying with my aunt in Windsor, then started hitchhiking, at first on my own, and then I met a guy in Florida.'

'You hitchhiked to Florida?'

'Well, yes, and took some Greyhounds, but I ended up in Tampa for about a year. I met my boyfriend Jeff there and we lived together for a year or so. He's the one who gave me the dragon tattoo.'

'He's a tattoo artist.'

'Yeah. When we broke up I made my way back here. Back to London. I lost all my weight during my transient years.'

'I don't remember you as being particularly fat.'

'Ha! Don't be ridiculous! I was a whale.'

'You aren't a whale now.'

'No, no I'm not. Do you like watching me dance?'

'I do.'

'I'm hot, aren't I?'

'Very.'

'You can touch me a little, you know.'

'That wouldn't be weird?'

'No, not at all.'

'Are you sure?'

'I want you to. Give me your hands ... Do you like that?'

'I do. Yes. Do you?'

'I do, a lot.'

'We've been in here for a few songs. How much do I owe you?'

'Don't worry about that now. Just enjoy. It's nice to see you again, Mark Phillips.'

'Thanks. It's a pleasure to meet you, Pamela.'

SIGISMUND MOHR:
THE MAN WHO BROUGHT
ELECTRICITY TO QUEBEC

'Je suis le souverain des choses transitoires.'
– from Count Montesquiou's *Les chauves-souris* (1893)

Money, a need for money, that's what led Sigismund Mohr – a Prussian immigrant, from Breslau to London to Montreal to Quebec City – to establish the City District Telegraph Company, which would lead Mohr to the Dominion Telegraph Company, the establishment of telegraph and telephone networks and, eventually, the first hydroelectric plant in Quebec. When Alexander Graham Bell bought up all the smaller telegraph and telephone companies in 1880 and was granted a cross-country long-distance monopoly, Mohr was hired as his agent in Quebec City, where he fulfilled his post successfully and dutifully, selling subscriptions and installing and improving upon the equipment, while tinkering with inventions of his own. The telephone caught on fast. But Mohr tired of working for Bell and in 1884 became director of the Quebec & Lévis Electric Light Company (Q&LEL Co.).

This is when he brought electricity to Quebec.

He initially set up a small thermal power station in the military warehouses near Port Saint-Jean in Quebec City. Bright electric light, powered by dynamos, started to replace gaslights.

The townspeople resented the plant greatly, however, with over a hundred inhabitants signing a petition for the disruptive power plant to be moved from the neighbourhood. He moved the plant to Montmorency Falls thirteen kilometres away, at the base of the falls and on a craggy bank, where the noise wouldn't bother anyone. For some, Mohr was a prophet, for others the Devil himself, and for others still yet another gifted engineer-slash-inventor in the age of gifted engineers-slash-inventors.

On September 2nd, 1889, he writes in his journal, *I try not to spend too much time thinking about Father Time, with his sandglass and sickle.* A friend and colleague, Charles Lemont, and Mohr had recently broken off their association at Q&LEL Co. Charles Lemont was politely asked to leave, though not by Mohr, according to Mohr's journal. Competitiveness, coupled with Charles's coveting of Mohr's wife, stained their friendship. *Charles was once a dear friend*, Mohr writes. And Mohr wasn't known to have many friends, as he was possessed of an obsessively industrious nature, though his industriousness wasn't always profitable; in fact, it wasn't until after 1880 that he finally started getting on top of his debts, his residence in Montreal having being condemned as *insalubrious* not a decade before. Eventually, he made some money, though not a fraction of the amounts of money that his ingenuity would make for others after his death on December 15th, 1893, from pneumonia, after going out two weeks earlier in a snowstorm to fix power lines at Montmorency Falls, the waterfalls he used to generate power for Quebec City, thirteen kilometres away, that is to say, the farthest electricity had hitherto travelled to power anything, let alone the city's port district.

Although Mohr was always in need of money, he was an impractical man, like many great inventors. He felt, as early as 1870, that he would one day make money, money earned from his creations – *Soon things will change*, he often said – though instead he found himself entangled in lawsuit after lawsuit for most of his adult life. His earnings went to debts and his family, lab and materials, and his efforts went on and on, without profit.

Mohr and his wife, Levi (née Blum, from New York), had five daughters – Philippine, Amelia, Lenorah, Fanny and Clara – and two sons: Eugene Philip and Henry Ralph. Despite financial strains, Mohr was a man of great concentration, a point his son Eugene Philip iterates in his memoir, *Days at Montmorency*, a short volume about the days leading up to Mohr's great exhibition of electric light on September 29th, 1885, in Quebec City, from Dufferin Terrace, when 20,000 people gathered after nightfall and cheered as he lit up thirty-four light stations. *By a signal given by Lieutenant Governor Louis-François-Rodrique Masson*, writes a journalist for the newspaper *Le Canadien, by means of an electric bell, the appearance of the terrace was transformed as if by a magic wand.* For the rest of the week, similar-sized crowds showed up to see Mohr light up the town *by means of transporting the fluid produced by Montmorency Falls to the thirty-four centres of light.* On the third night of his exhibition, in a moment of improvised showmanship, Mohr cut the current, then restored it immediately; the paper reports, *The crowd erupted in applause.*

Luciferian in the dark night, with his wild silver hair, moustache and muttonchops, Mohr stood on the terrace, controlling all the fire-like light. The crowd stood and stared, rapt. And the electric light lit up moisture coming out of the tens of thousands of townspeople's mouths; the fog floated in the air, suspended in the light – that is, charged, shifting and coruscating, as if the light were holding the vapour before it evaporated into the cold night air.

According to Eugene Philip's memoir, Mohr was attacked later that night; while being congratulated by many, a drunken sailor accused him of performing *the Devil's work* and took a swing at Mohr, who was ushered away by many, the sailor taken in the opposite direction. *No trouble*, Mohr said. *No trouble*. The sailor shouted, *Sacrilège!*

Mohr's Jewishness made some skeptical of him and some outright violent, though it didn't help that his wife and daughters sold fancy lingerie in a store at 105, rue Saint-Jean, beside their home at 103, rue Saint-Jean. The Mohr family were outsiders par excellence, bringing modernity to the fortified city where the St. Lawrence River narrows.

Many who socialized with Mohr saw him as a maunderer, aimless and fanciful, even incoherent. But after his light exhibition, even they started to see Mohr differently. Eugene Philip writes, *Some old friends were hostile toward Papa but he was possessed with his work; most of his friends were in awe of him.* Mohr was befriended by Cyrille Duquet, a local jeweller, who also invented the double-ended telephone handset. The two would occasionally dine together and Duquet would take Mohr out on his sailboat and they'd visit his power station by the falls from time to time.

Your electricity will soon power everything, said Duquet.

That is my hope, Mohr said. *And it will be inexpensive, for everyone.*

Mohr writes in his journal, *All things celestial and terrestrial fascinate me. The constant motion. Nonetheless*, Mysterium Tremendum – *the cosmos scares the living daylights out of me, too.* Absque hoc nihil est – *apart from this there is nothing.*

Mohr read voraciously, according to Eugene Philip. He wrote in his journals, too, almost every night at a small writing desk with a tallow candle and an inkstand, and later in life the soft candlelight was replaced by dim lamplight, and he'd look out his window from his writing desk at the lampposts in the street with great satisfaction, though he didn't live to publish a book about his work and discoveries. For all intents and purposes, Mohr has been lost to history — that is to say, he's not a celebrated figure in Quebec history, or the larger story of Canadian history, either, or the still larger history of electricity, too. His name is almost as anonymous, now, as the names of the labourers who helped his vision come to pass. Although Mohr did much of the work himself, he needed a large crew to clear an area, deracinate the trees, and help expand and build his new plant at the base of the waterfalls, replacing the old Patterson-Hall factory he'd been using, a factory that once produced broomsticks. He would spend more and more time at the plant site than at home. Nonetheless, he loved his family dearly; they're mentioned on almost every page of his extant journals.

Mohr didn't live to see the inauguration of his new power station at the base of Montmorency, in 1894. Regardless, his last years were filled with success. There were always those, however, who were suspicious and perhaps resentful of Mohr's achievements, like Charles Baillairgé, who initiated an inquiry into Mohr's company in 1891, believing that he was overcharging the City of Quebec for its lamps. *Mohr is a menace*, Baillairgé told a reporter for *Le Canadien, who is exploiting our city and profiting for himself.* The results of the inquiry, to Baillairgé's chagrin, were in favour of the Q&LEL Co.: Mohr was producing less costly and more efficient energy than all of his competitors in the city, it was determined, and perhaps on the entire continent. This made him an enemy of the Quebec Gas Company, who had been losing their hold on the city's energy contracts to the Q&LEL Co. for years.

Mohr followed the work of Nikola Tesla closely, and only one year after Tesla and George Westinghouse had patented his alternating current (AC) generator, the Q&LEL Co. was also producing AC, switching early on from direct current (DC) to AC, siding with Tesla/Westinghouse, over Thomas Alva Edison and DC, for which Edison held all the patents, during the so-called War of the Currents. *I admire Tesla greatly*, Mohr writes, *and believe alternating current will eventually bring electricity to every household.* AC could travel farther distances, was more efficient, and ended up being invaluable in creating Quebec City's urban electrical grid. Mohr, moreover, would improve upon Tesla's generator and by 1892, when commencing construction of the new and expanded plant at Montmorency, his three 600-kw AC generators were purported to be the first of their kind.

These generators will soon be used everywhere, he told his son.

Eugene Philip writes, Ora et labora *was my father's motto but he neglected the* ora. Mohr's apostasy was noted by his wife, Levi, who was active with Beth Israel, the small Jewish community formally established in the 1850s. Jews had been in Quebec since the mid-18th century; prior to 1759, however, Jews weren't welcome in New France, as it was for Catholics only, but Jews arrived with the British. Mohr wasn't particularly interested in matters of Judaism, though he felt some vestigial attachment to the community, for many of its members were from Breslau like him.

Electricity, energy, of course, had become his muse – inexpensive clean energy, which he knew how to provide – and his vision became more refined as time went on. But then time ran out – that is, when Mohr had really hit his stride and established himself as the father of electricity in Quebec and, therefore, in the rest of Canada, he soon gave up the ghost.

Cyrille Duquet describes Mohr in his memoir, *Remarques envers l'alchimie*, as a sort of modest soothsayer or prophet, the alchemic master Duquet longed to be, though Mohr wasn't transmuting lead into gold but rather water into light. *Everything's energy,* Mohr remarked to Duquet, *but of course you know that.* Although Duquet writes very warmly about Mohr, he emphasizes that he was opaque to both kith and kin; Duquet writes about commenting on a painting in Mohr's house, a painting of pinkish chrysanthemums, which was a gift from Mohr's former colleague, Charles Lemont, to Mohr's wife, Levi – a species of flower she'd never seen. Mohr went silent when Duquet said how lovely he thought the painting was and, Duquet writes, he remained silent for the remainder of the luncheon.

The night Mohr caught pneumonia, two weeks before he died, he was walking through the snow on his way home to 103, rue Saint-Jean, and he saw a series of his lamps go out. Immediately, he knew a line was down and had a sense of where the problem was. There was a line by the plant, by the falls, that swayed wildly in the wind, and the wind was picking up in the snowstorm. When he arrived home he saddled his horse and left for the falls without telling anyone. The horse's hooves clopped on the cobblestones and splashed through the puddles. It hadn't snowed in days and now it was coming down strong. Mohr winced in the snow and picked up speed when he was out of the port district on horseback.

When he arrived at the falls, the line was in the water. He needed to reconnect it to the plant, but it meant going into the water and taking it out of the water first with a long wooden pole, then dragging it to shore. The horse was half-submerged in the water and its body looked oily, as if the horse were wading through tar, not water. The snow made the moon invisible. He got the line and dragged it out, then climbed the steps on the side of the plant while holding it, since it was inactive and all the generators were down, and he reconnected it to the side of the building. It didn't take him that long, he later told Eugene Philip. But the cold and the snow made him sick. His boots and legs were wet from the river and when he returned to 103, rue Saint-Jean, his daughters and wife were worried and shocked by his appearance.

They couldn't believe the state he was in, according to Eugene Philip, returning home with wet boots and his legs shaking and his teeth chattering and his silver muttonchops and moustache filled with snow and small icicles. Amelia and Lenorah boiled water for a bath as Levi stripped him of his clothes in their bedroom. The sixty-six-year-old Mohr knew that he'd been out in the wet and cold for too long, as he shivered before his wife. She wrapped him in blankets and brought him to their tub, while the girls poured in bucket after bucket of boiling water. The steam filled the room, fogging up the small mirror and walls, as Mohr lay in the tub with his eyes shut. Eugene Philip writes, *It was as if he were contemplating the mistake he had made. He knew he had been out in the cold for far too long, riding his horse in the snow, so as to restore the light.*

He was bedridden for two weeks before the pneumonia killed him.

In that time, in addition to Mohr's doctor, Dr. Maurice Benoit, Duquet visited him several times. Mohr was unresponsive, for the most part, when his friend spoke to him, though Duquet returned again and again. *The Mohr household was filled*, Duquet writes, *with all the terrifying miserable excitement of being close to death.* Mohr's unresponsiveness was partly due to a small daily dose of opium prescribed by the doctor and prepared by the apothecary, though both Duquet and Eugene Philip said he looked meditative.

Duquet writes of being with Mohr a year earlier, on the landing stairs where his sailboat was docked, surrounded by cloud-capped hills, a fleur-de-lis painted on his sailboat's bow, the loose white sail flapping in the wind as the men talked under a blue sky. Duquet writes that Mohr was excited about the construction of his new plant and at the time, by 1892, he knew he'd accomplished something great.

After Mohr's death on December 15th, 1893, the whole Mohr family moved to New York – that is, where Levi was born and where much of the Blum family still lived – bringing Mohr's body with them to receive proper Jewish funeral rites. The family didn't want his grave to be in Quebec City, where they wouldn't be able to visit. So Sigismund Mohr was buried in New York. In 1894, a little more than a decade after the completion of the Brooklyn Bridge, Eugene Philip followed in his father's footsteps and began a lifelong career running a telegraph-and-electricity company in Brooklyn.

While Mohr lay dying, Eugene Philip writes that he would recount to his father stories of the nights on Dufferin Terrace, when Mohr put on his electric-light exhibitions for the first time, drawing tens of thousands of townspeople. His father shallowly breathing, Eugene Philip reminded him of all the vapour illuminated and trapped in the light in the night air.

What you did was incredible, Papa, he said. *To have suspended something as transitory as breath.*

HIC ET UBIQUE

We stood at baggage claim at Jomo Kenyatta International Airport – that is, Boris, the Russian photographer; Tanya, his eight-year-old daughter; and me, the journalist – waiting for god knows how long by the carousel for my suitcase. Theirs appeared at the top of the carousel immediately, but my suitcase didn't seem to have made it from Montreal to Amsterdam to Nairobi. Boris's daughter, Tanya, was irritated that her father was making her wait for my luggage to arrive, even though she'd had hers for going on twenty minutes and her grandparents were waiting on the other side of the gate, eager to see their granddaughter, who they rarely got to see, as they lived in Nairobi and she in Montreal. I felt terrible.

'Boris,' I said, 'seriously, go on without me. I'll catch up.'
'No, no,' he said. 'It's your first time. I'm not leaving you.'
'Dad,' said Tanya, 'let's go let's go let's go!'
'No, Tanya, we'll only be a minute. Don't be rude.'
'I want to see Grandma and Papa.'
'You have to wait. It won't be long,' he said.

But he was wrong. My suitcase didn't appear for another fifteen minutes and by then we were all covered in sweat, our clothes soaked through, and weary from the flights, two eight-hour ordeals, with a seven-hour layover between the first and the second in the Amsterdam airport, where we rented a day-room for approximately five hours, so as to lie down for a bit and shower between flights.

My suitcase was broken when I pulled it off the carousel: it only had one wheel now and there was a large crack in the plastic panel that braced the bottom.

Boris said, 'Don't worry, man. We'll get you a new suitcase while we're here. They're very inexpensive here. We'll get a better suitcase.'

'Sounds good,' I said, and swallowed. Other than the fact that I couldn't stop sweating, it felt like I'd left my corporeality somewhere in the sky between Amsterdam and Nairobi. Things seemed out of focus.

Tanya screamed, '*Babushka! Papa!*' as her grandparents gathered her up in a hug, the babushka a stout but attractive Russian woman, with a large bosom that absorbed her grandchild, and the papa a tall man, a man of Maasai origins, from the Rift Valley, but he'd been living in Nairobi for fifty-five years, he told me on the car ride from the airport to his home, where he worked as an engineer, though he travelled for work a lot, and in fact he had to take the bus to Mombasa in the morning; he was working on a beachfront hotel development there.

'How did you two meet?' I asked them on the car ride, and Martin, the papa, told me that he met Galina, the babushka, in 1966, a couple of years after the independent Republic of Kenya was formed, while he was studying in Leningrad, in the former Soviet Union. Shortly after Kenyan independence, both the United States and the Soviet Union started offering many different types of scholarships in Kenya, Martin told me as he drove, Tanya and Galina and our luggage and me packed into the back of his Toyota hatchback, Boris seated beside his father-in-law, as Martin worked the gearshift from time to time, putting his whole tall body into it.

'So I'd gotten a scholarship to study in Leningrad,' continued Martin, 'and that's where I met Galina, at the Herzen University, where she was studying engineering, too.'

'Oh wow,' I said, turning to Galina, who I was pressed up against, who had Tanya on her lap, squeezing her grand-daughter tightly, and Tanya glowed with happiness. 'You're an engineer, too.'

'I was in the Soviet Union,' Galina said. 'But not here.'

'She doesn't work,' said Martin.

'I raised your children and now Sveta's child, also.'

'I need to make the money,' he added. 'To give to her.'

I looked out the windows, gathering impressions of the outskirts of Nairobi, but jetlagged impressions, somewhat surreal; the land and sky looked flattened and overexposed, like in an old colour photograph, as we drove from the airport to Martin and Galina's house. I was booked at a hotel, the Heron Court Hotel, but everyone insisted that I come over for dinner first. Boris and Tanya were staying with Galina and Martin, though Boris and I were leaving for the coast later in the week. Tanya would stay on with her grandparents till we returned. In the meantime, I'd stay at the Heron Court Hotel.

When we arrived at Martin and Galina's house, first Martin had to get out and remove a padlock from a gate, which swung open onto their small neighbourhood. He pulled the car past the gate and into their laneway and then got out and ran back to close and lock the gate. I got out and unpacked the luggage from the hatchback and proceeded to follow Galina, carrying the bags into her house in a few trips.

'I need to lie down,' said Boris. 'I'm sure John does, too.'

'I'm okay,' I said, not wanting to impose, though I could hardly imagine staying awake.

Boris laughed. 'Man, we've been travelling for two days basically. You're tired. Lie down till supper.'

'There's a room upstairs,' said Galina. 'Alexi's room. You can lie down there for now.'

'Who's Alexi?' I asked, impulsively, immediately worrying that I'd asked something I shouldn't have.

'My grandson,' said Galina. 'Tanya's cousin.'

'He's Svetlana's son,' said Boris. 'Sveta's my sister-in-law.'

'Oh,' I said.

'Sveta lives here now, too,' said Galina. 'She's been having problems with her boyfriend. Tyson.'

'Tyson's all right,' said Martin, waving off his wife's worries. 'Just a man.'

I didn't say anything but Galina and I shared a look, a mother conveying her worry, me conveying my understanding that relationships are complicated and difficult and hopefully everything would be okay, or at least that's what I was trying to convey with my bleary jetlagged expression.

I said, 'Do you mind if I take a quick shower before I lie down?'

There was no way I could lie on a bed that wasn't mine in the state I was in. The clothes I'd been travelling in were beyond ripe, having been sweated in for far too long, and I really wasn't feeling well.

'Yes,' said Galina. 'I'll get you a towel.'

'Thank you,' I said. 'I really appreciate it.'

I dug out fresh clothes and my toiletry kit from my suitcase and took them to the bathroom. I took off my clothes and looked at my livid left arm; the inoculations I'd gotten at the Tropical Disease Centre at the Royal Victoria Hospital in Montreal had left my arm black and blue and purple and brown and yellow and it was tender to the touch. I showered quickly, cleaned any trace of me from the bathroom save the lingering steam and consequent humidity, then went upstairs and lay down in the boy's bedroom. Although I often find falling asleep very difficult, I was out within five minutes. Dead to the world.

I was woken up by Alexi, a shirtless three-year-old boy, who walked into the room and poked me several times. I woke with a start and at first had no idea where I was. The boy didn't seem startled by my being startled, and he simply stared at me as I wiped my eyes and said, 'Hi there, little man.'

I heard Galina yell, 'John! We've put tea out! Come join us!'

'Coming,' I said, my voice raspy. 'Thank you, Galina,' I added.

There was nothing in the world I wanted to do more than keep sleeping; in fact, I'm not sure I've ever slept so deeply as I did for the forty-odd minutes I slept before being awoken by Alexi and beckoned by Galina.

My head was heavy as I walked down the stairs, following the small child. Boris was sitting with his father-in-law discussing politics – Kenyan politics, Russian politics, U.S. politics – while drinking tea and eating sugar cookies. I sat down with them at the circular dining room table and Galina quickly put a cup and saucer before me, dropped a teabag in the cup and poured in boiling water from a kettle.

'Sugar?' she said. '*Moloko*? I mean, milk?'

I said no thank you but she put in a teaspoonful of sugar anyway, so I said *spasiba* and smiled at her. '*Pozhalujsta*,' she said.

We munched on sugar cookies and I listened while Boris and Martin talked – about next year's elections in Kenya, about Vladimir Putin, about the presidential elections on the horizon in the United States, even though they were two years away – but then eventually, when Galina sat down, after serving us all, she started asking questions about me. *Where are you from?* she asked. And I answered Canada: originally I'm from outside a medium-sized city called London, in Ontario, but now I live in Montreal, in Quebec, I said, where Boris and Nina live with Tanya. *Are you married?* she asked. I said no but I have a girlfriend. Galina smiled. *What's her name, the girlfriend?* Galina asked. Stacey, I said. *Do you live together?* she asked. Not yet, I said, but we've been together for almost five years.

I didn't express any of my insecurities with respect to my relationship with Stacey; it didn't feel appropriate, obviously, but my misgivings dominated my mind.

We talked briefly about how Boris ended up with Nina, their daughter, who'd travelled to the U.S. to go to Union College in Schenectady, in upstate New York, on a scholarship, where Boris was a visiting lecturer, originally from Leningrad, but he'd lived stateside for many years, and there met Nina.

'How did you meet Boris and Nina?' asked Galina.

'I met Boris at a birthday party for a common friend, a Croatian-American writer, Marko, and we hit it off and decided we'd try and work together one day,' I said. 'I was aware of Boris as a photographer before we'd met at Marko's party.'

'He's very good,' said Martin, with pride.

'One of the best!'

'We even have a setup here, a little darkroom out back for Boris in the addition,' said Martin, 'for when he visits. There's a steel cot and a toilet in there, too. We call it Boris's Place. No one else ever goes in there. When you're not here, Boris, it's totally empty. I won't let anyone touch anything.'

'It's okay,' said Boris. 'You can use the space.'

'No,' said Martin. 'I don't want anyone damaging your equipment or the kids messing with the chemicals or your computer equipment, either.'

'*Spasiba*,' said Boris.

'*Pozhalujsta*,' Martin said. 'I need some more hot water, Galina.'

And Galina went to the kitchen for the kettle.

After another cup of tea, Martin suggested that we move the party outside for a drink.

Martin, Boris and I sat at a table in the backyard, where Martin had produced a large bottle of Stolichnaya from an old Coca-Cola cooler and three small green glass bottles of lime soda. We drank the vodka from shot glasses, Russian style, and we sipped the lime soda on the side. Martin said, holding up his shot glass, 'John, to your first trip to Kenya!'

'Cheers! Thank you for your hospitality,' I said and we all clinked glasses and took back the viscous vodka.

Tanya returned with a plate of barbecued chicken and a bottle of hot sauce, a large bowl of brown rice and peas, vegetable samosas, salad and bread. We stopped drinking vodka while we ate. I wasn't hungry, though the food was very good and I ate a little of everything so as not to insult my generous hosts. The sun was setting and it was beautiful in the backyard. The large sky was turning dark at the edges but colourful still in the centre – purple and pink and blue and pale yellow. There was a cool breeze fluttering the leaves on the bushes and trees.

Boris said, 'Man, it's like being in a Italian film. Look at the sky! Look at the colours!'

And it was true. There's nothing like the magic hour in a backyard in Nairobi, sitting with great company, drinking vodka and eating barbecue.

Still, I didn't feel right. Even though the temperature had dropped – due to its high altitude, Nairobi's cool in the evenings – I was sweating heavily and asked to be excused to use the washroom.

'There's a toilet in Boris's Place,' Martin said. 'It's just right there.' He pointed toward the small addition attached to the back of the main house.

I stood and walked to the washroom, where I splashed water on my ghostly face for several minutes. I wanted to drink the water from my cupped hands but was worried about giardia, about the possibility of getting sicker. Underneath my eyes was black, and my unshaved face looked sallow. My forehead wouldn't stop perspiring – I was a perspiring ghost, I thought, even though now it was cool outside.

When I returned to the party, Martin had resumed the vodka drinking, and there was a young woman sitting at the table now, too, in her late twenties or early thirties.

'This is Sveta,' Boris said. 'Nina's sister.'

'Nice to meet you. I'm John.'

'Nice to meet you, John,' she said and smiled.

'John's a writer from Montreal,' said Boris, 'a friend of mine and Nina's. He's covering the festival.'

I sat down beside her, in my original seat, and she poured me a shot of vodka. I thanked her, clinked my small glass to hers, and drank it back. I reached for a drumstick from the platter. I figured with all the drinking, and the travelling, I should probably eat a little more, even though I felt feverish. Feed a cold, starve a fever, I thought. But nevertheless I found myself chewing on the drumstick. I asked Sveta to pass the hot sauce. She laughed and passed it to me.

'What's so funny,' I said. 'Isn't the hot sauce good?'

'No, it's good,' Sveta said. 'It's just, well ... '

'Well what?'

'It's a little crude,' she said. 'But my boyfriend and I say that before eating this hot sauce it's a good idea to put the toilet paper in the freezer.'

We both laughed and I poured a very modest amount of the hot sauce onto my plate. 'I'll be careful,' I said.

Alexi ran over and grabbed at his mother's leg, crying, and she picked the boy up and patted his back.

Martin waved his hand in exasperation. 'Stop coddling the boy,' he said. 'The boy cries too much.' He looked at me and shook his head.

'He's fine, Papa,' Sveta said. And she carried the boy inside, away from the table.

'It's important for Alexi to learn to be a man,' said Martin. 'He's surrounded by too many women.'

Boris said, 'All right, guys, one more shot and then I have to go to bed.'

He filled three shot glasses, said *cheers*, and we drank back the vodka.

'Make sure John gets to the hotel okay,' said Boris, as he walked toward his room.

'I will,' said Martin.

'Don't worry about me,' I said. 'I'll just grab a cab and I'll be fine.'

Both Boris and Martin laughed.

Boris said, 'Look, man, it's your first time in Nairobi and it's nighttime. We've been drinking. You can't just hail a cab.'

'I'll call my driver Billy,' said Martin. 'Billy Mutinda. Billy will take care of him. I'll ride with John.'

'Oh, no, you don't have to do that!' I said. 'If we just call Billy, that's good. I don't need an escort.'

'We've been drinking a lot,' said Boris. 'Martin will see you to the hotel.'

'I don't want to put you out.'

I felt like an encumbrance, and I was anxious to recuperate alone.

'No, no, not a problem,' said Martin. 'I'll get Billy to drop me at the bus station anyway,' he added. 'I have to go to Mombasa. I'll pack a bag and take the night bus.'

'How long is the bus ride?' I asked.

'About seven hours,' said Martin. 'Maybe a little longer.'

'Oh wow. That's long,' I said, surprised.

'I'll sleep,' said Martin.

'All right, guys, goodnight,' said Boris.

'Goodnight,' I said.

I went to the living room and all the lights were off. I searched for my suitcase in the dark and gathered my gear and carried it out the front door, not rolling the broken suitcase, moving as quietly as I could. They must've put the boy to bed, I thought, and waited for Martin outside.

It was dark out now and a beautiful night and I was excited to be in Nairobi and my blood was charged with surfeit vodka shots. I looked up at the starry sky and took the night air deep into my lungs. I felt very free, standing with my suitcase, waiting for Martin and Billy Mutinda, the driver.

Martin came out the front door carrying a small brown leather bag and clapped me on the back. 'You're swaying a little,' he said. 'Good thing you have your suitcase to prop you up!' And he laughed good-naturedly, resting his hand on my shoulder, towering above me.

A small grey Mitsubishi sedan pulled up to the gate and Martin said, 'Aha! Here's Billy!'

He opened the gate and Billy got out of the car and greeted us.

'Billy,' said Martin. 'My son-in-law Boris is in town. This is his friend John.'

'Hi, John,' said Billy.

I said *hi* back.

'I want you to look after Boris,' said Martin.

'Okay, yes, yes,' said Billy.

'And I want you to take care of John,' said Martin.

Billy smiled.

He packed our luggage into the back and we set off for the hotel.

'Is the hotel far?' I asked.

'No,' said Martin. 'Maybe fifteen minutes.'

He talked to Billy in Kiswahili and they both laughed and I looked out the windows but the night outside seemed blurry, though I knew we were still on the outskirts of the city, making our way closer to the lights. There were a series of churches with their crucifixes climbing skyward on a stretch of road before the hotel.

Soon we pulled up to a high black steel gate, where a security guard in a white shirt stood before the U-shaped laneway to the hotel's entrance.

Martin informed the guard that I was a guest staying at the hotel and the security guard peered into the car and looked at me and I waved and he went in his little booth and automatically opened a section of the gate. Billy pulled up to the entrance under a concrete canopy, with a skylight. He hopped out of the car and unloaded my luggage and Martin let me out and said to Billy, 'Give John your number. So he can call you if he needs a car.'

Billy dipped into the driver's seat and emerged extending a business card toward me. 'Call me,' he said. I took it and closed an eye to focus on it – there was a rather accurate cartoon of Billy's Mitsubishi on the card and his name, *Billy Mutinda*, and below his name it read *For All Your Drivings Needs ...*

'If I find out you didn't take care of my son-in-law and John,' said Martin to Billy, 'I'll kill you!'

And they both laughed and piled into the car. A valet approached me and put his hand on my suitcase and Martin said from the passenger-side window, 'Okay, it looks like you're set.'

'Thank you so much, Martin, for everything,' I said.

'No problem,' he said. 'Good luck. Enjoy Nairobi! I'll see you when I get back from Mombasa.'

'Bye,' I said and waved to them as the security guard opened the gate and the car pulled away from the Heron Court Hotel.

The concierge, a handsome older gentleman in a blue suit with round steel glasses, smiled at me from behind the high front desk as I fumbled for my passport, then handed it over. A portrait of President Kibaki looked down on us.

He typed on his computer for what seemed like a long time and I took notice of the bar and restaurant to the right of the lobby, which was fairly happening, I thought.

'How late is the bar open?' I said.

'It'll be open till at least midnight tonight. Perhaps later if it is busy,' said the concierge.

'And it's ten o'clock now.'

'That's right, sir,' he said.

'I might check it out,' I said, pointing barward.

'Excellent, sir, everything seems fine,' he said, passing the passport back to me with my room keys. 'You're in room 229. Just up the stairs, walk outside, and turn left at the swimming pool. It's three rooms in.'

'Okay,' I said.

'We'll have your bags brought to your room for you, if you'd like to visit the bar.'

'That sounds good,' I said. 'Thanks.'

'*Asante sana*,' he said. 'Thank you very much.'

There was a washroom to the side of the lobby, which I visited before hitting the bar. I washed my face again and confronted myself in the large mirror. I was still perspiring, though the alcohol had buttressed me a little; there was a little more colour in my face. I decided I'd drink one beer, so as to get my bearings, but no more than one. I figured it'd do me good, a cleansing ale. Then, bedtime.

I walked into the restaurant and passed the tables and diners and walked up a few steps to an elevated bar with several high barstools surrounding it. I awkwardly climbed onto one and said hello to the young gentleman behind the bar.

'What kind of beer do you have?' I asked.

'We have Pilsner and Tusker.'

'What's the difference?'

'They are both lagers. There isn't much difference but I prefer Pilsner.'

'Then Pilsner it is!'

He produced a large perspiring bottle from a small fridge behind the bar, popped the cap off with an opener and placed it in front of me on a Tusker coaster, and then he gave me a glass, too. I paid in Kenyan shillings and drank from the bottle.

I drank that bottle and then ordered another and moved to a nearby table to watch cars pull up to the front entrance and the people attending the literary festival get out, with their suitcases and knapsacks, looking somewhat dazed from the travel. Ostensibly, that's why Boris and I were in Nairobi — to attend a literary festival. But really Boris had been trying to convince me to come with him for years. We just needed an excuse.

Boris was taking the photos and I was writing an article. We'd pitched the idea to a magazine in Canada, that is, an article about East Africa's arts scene, especially putting emphasis on its thriving literary scene, using this festival as impetus, a festival put on by a number of organizations, including a Kenyan literary journal, the University of Nairobi and a few foundations, et cetera. Anyway, there would be good writers and various artists kicking around so it made sense to write a piece. And the magazine loved the idea. Boris was already a de facto member of Nairobi's arts scene, visiting the country usually once a year, though every time he came back he became more and more involved with local artists. This festival was a great reason to visit and the magazine was covering most of our expenses.

My head in hand, leaning my right elbow on the tabletop, I closed one eye so as to make out who was entering the hotel. My friend Mark, a poet from Chicago, would be attending, so I kept my one eye peeled for him. He'd emailed me saying he was getting in around midnight, but I didn't see him yet and my second big beer was almost done.

I slowly finished the beer and then decided it was time to call it a night. Besides, the restaurant had stopped serving food a while ago and the bar crowd was thinning out. But then I decided to drink one more beer for the road. It was a poor decision, but I was strangely too jacked up for bed, even though I was beyond tired and full of alcohol.

At some point I felt a little sick to my stomach and left without finishing the third Pilsner.

When I went out to the lobby I was staggering a little. I'd lost my bearings. A young porter walked by and I asked him where was room 229, looking at the number engraved in my brass key. He said kindly, 'Just this way, sir. Follow me.'

We walked past the pool and I stayed away from its edge – it was lit up underwater and looked electric blue with bright light. It was a bit of a blur.

The porter got me to my door and I pulled out a wadded-up five-dollar U.S. bill I had in my jeans pocket and he refused to take it, laughing, smiling, so I said *thank you* and he kindly unlocked my door for me. Then, again I asked him to take the money and he did.

I closed the door and locked it and fell down on the bed. I lay there, supine, staring up at the ceiling, looking at its bumpy texture. Breathing heavily, I saw the TV high up in the left-hand corner of the room, tucked right up against the ceiling, suspended by chains. The remote was on the bedside table, so I turned it on.

Charlie Chaplin's *The Kid* was playing and I felt relieved. The movie had just begun.

I propped myself up against the wall with a pillow, as there was no headboard.

The story's about a woman – *whose sin was motherhood.* She has a baby boy and the father, an artist, isn't in the picture. She can't afford to care for the child, so she leaves him in the backseat of a fancy car, with a note: *Please love and care for this orphan child.*

Shortly after she leaves the child, however, some car thieves happen upon the luxury automobile and decide to steal it but then discover the infant in the backseat. They decide to leave the baby with some trash in a nearby alleyway, where later the Tramp finds him.

Unsuccessfully, the Tramp tries to rid himself of the baby, but when he reads the note – *Please love and care for this orphan child* – he decides to accept his fate as the infant's guardian and he names him John, caring for him from babyhood to boyhood, but eventually the adorable little boy is taken from the Tramp by the ruthless authorities and both the boy and the Tramp wail for one another as they're forcibly separated.

I choked up a little. I was exhausted and full of alcohol and vaccinations and more emotional than usual. When the Tramp is reunited with the boy, and they embrace tightly, crying, cheek to cheek, in portrait, I, too, felt like crying but didn't. Instead, I started to fade off to the soothing rhythms of the black-and-white silent-era film.

The morning came fast and I hadn't drawn the curtains and my room was full of sunlight and lightly playing gospel music. I'd left the TV on and some sort of religious programming was playing. I checked my watch and it was only six a.m.

I turned off the TV and went to wash up. In the mirror, my face looked sallower than the day before, my face looked more unshaven, and below my eyes looked blacker. I betrayed an undeniable ghostliness. I turned on the shower and got in the small tiled stall.

The hot water felt good and the washroom filled with steam. I washed my body hard and my face, too, trying to stimulate blood flow, though I washed my livid left arm gently, examining it and deciding that it was more yellow than black so it must be healing – slowly, but healing, I thought. No cause for concern.

When I got out of the shower I opened the washroom window, cranking open some glass flaps, so as to let out some steam, and I wiped down the mirror before brushing my teeth and shaving. I had no bottled water but I figured it was safe to brush my teeth with tap water. Even after shaving and washing up, I still looked sick and tired.

I returned to the room proper in only a towel and unpacked some books and put them on the windowsill. I took one, P. G. Wodehouse's *The Inimitable Jeeves*, a gift from a friend, and lay back down on the bed to read some familiar stories of the great butler Jeeves and his charge, Bertie Wooster, the ultimate gentleman of leisure.

When Boris saw me reading the Wodehouse stories on one of the flights, after he, Tanya and I had all watched *Talladega Nights: The Ballad of Ricky Bobby*, a Will Ferrell movie, on our respective screens on the backs of the headrests in front of us, he'd said: 'Oh, Wodehouse is great!' Then, adding, 'We're never more nostalgic than we are for a time that never existed.'

After a half-hour of reading, the pleasant and funny stories lulled me back to sleep for about an hour, and when I woke again I figured the restaurant would now be open and I could get some bottled water and a cup of tea. I was tremendously thirsty, with all the travel and the drinks. So I rose and dressed and put on sunglasses and went to go check out the restaurant.

The hotel was sort of an open concept – as soon I exited my room, I was outside, and then I turned to my left and walked by a couple of rooms and then I was at the outdoor pool, which in daylight looked inviting, more so than in my memory, and I turned right at the pool, walked down a few steps, and then was in the lobby, which I bypassed for the restaurant.

When I entered the restaurant, a young man in a white shirt and black slacks immediately asked me if I was there for breakfast. I said yes. Breakfast was included with the room. He asked me if I wanted to sit inside or outside and I said outside. He walked me to a terrace out front of the restaurant, a fenced-off area filled with tables and chairs, plants and flowers, to the side of the hotel's entrance. I was seated in a wicker-bottom chair and thanked him and looked at the menu.

There were three choices of complimentary breakfast: one, a pancake, a sausage, with sliced mango and pineapple; two, yogurt and granola, with berries, and sliced mango and pineapple; or, three, eggs, sausage, potatoes, with sliced mango and pineapple. All breakfasts came with coffee or tea, toast, with jam packets and butter packets, and a small glass of orange juice.

I was impressed – it all looked pretty good.

A waiter approached, another young man dressed similarly to the maître d', and brightly said, '*Hujambo, bwana?* How are you today, sir?'

'*Sijambo*,' I said, remembering the phrase from the back section of the Kenya *Lonely Planet*. 'It's a very beautiful morning,' I added.

'It is,' the waiter said. His name tag said Robert.

'My name's John,' I said.

'Nice to meet you, John. I'm Robert,' he said, making no motion to his name tag, and then he added, 'Would you like some coffee or tea?'

'Tea would be great,' I said. 'And I'll have a bottle of water, too, please.'

'Not a problem, sir. But the bottled water isn't included with the breakfast.'

'That's fine,' I said.

'Do you know what you'd like for breakfast?'

'I'll try number one,' I said, 'with the pancake.'

'I'll bring you your tea and water,' he said and was gone.

Cars continued to pull up to the entrance and drop off staggering travellers. Robert returned with a small steel teapot with a teabag in it, a ceramic saucer and mug, some sugar packets, a shot glass of milk, a bottle of water and a glass.

'*Asante sana*,' I said.

'*Karibu*,' he said. 'Your breakfast will be right out.'

'Thanks.'

Breakfast was good. I ate most of it, then asked Robert for the bill for the water, which I paid for in shillings and left a tip.

In the lobby a line of people stood waiting to get to the front desk, where the same concierge from the night before checked them in, one party at a time. They looked hot and tired and I sympathized, but I was more surprised that the same concierge who was working at ten o'clock the night before was manning the desk at nine-thirty a.m. He looked dapper, too, and very fresh. I didn't feel fresh at all.

I felt a slap on my back.

'How's it going, man?'

I turned around and my friend Mark was grinning, his

hair wet.

'Mark!' I said. And we briefly hugged.

'When did you get in?' I said.

'Last night, around midnightish.'

'Ha,' I said. 'I drank a few beers at the bar, thinking I might catch you, but then I sort of faded off.'

'Yeah,' he said, laughing, 'I saw you sitting at a table when I was checking in. You looked like you were falling asleep. I wanted to come in and say hello but I had to hit the rack. I was a zombie, too, and couldn't drink.'

'Oh, man, how embarrassing,' I said. 'Yeah, Boris's father-in-law got us a little drunk upon arrival, doing vodka shots in his backyard.'

'Nice,' said Mark. 'Sounds like fun.'

'Yeah, I mean, it was fun. But after twenty-four hours of travel probably inadvisable.'

'Of course,' said Mark. 'But you're in one piece.'

'Sort of. I don't want to ruin the trip with hangovers.'

'Have you had breakfast?' he said.

'I just did.'

'Oh too bad,' he said.

'I'm just going to head back to my room but we'll catch up in a bit,' I said.

'Sounds good.'

'Enjoy your breakfast,' I said. 'It's good!'

When I got back to my room I brushed my teeth again, after having put corn syrup on my pancake, and took my anti-malarial medication, which I'd been taking in the mornings after eating a little breakfast. Nairobi doesn't have a malaria problem, but the island I was heading to, Lamu, is in a malarious region, so I took the pills in preparation.

Then my bedside phone rang, which startled me.

I picked up and it was a young woman saying that a Mr. Boris was in the lobby, waiting for me. I'd be right there, I told the woman on the phone.

Boris was sitting on a red velvet upholstered bench reading the *Standard*, when I walked the few steps down into lobby. He spotted me right away and stood up, folding the news-paper and setting it on the coffee table in front of him.

'How's it going?' he said.

'Good,' I said.

He patted me on the back.

'You got here okay,' he said.

'Yes, Martin made sure I got in all right. He's terrific, a very nice man. And he and Billy were funny; he told Billy that if he didn't look after us he'd kill him.'

'Ha,' said Boris. 'That won't be necessary, I don't think.'

'How're you?' I said.

'Good,' he said. 'But I've booked myself a room here till we go to Lamu. I talked to Anita, and she gave me a room. This way, too, I can just be here where everybody will be and take the odd photo for the piece.'

'It'll be more convenient,' I said.

'Yeah, this way I don't have to take cars constantly,' he said. 'It'll be easier, and Tanya's having a great time with her cousin and aunt and grandparents.'

'Sounds good,' I said.

'We should head into town and pick up cellphones,' he said. 'They're inexpensive and it'll make communicating so much easier. That way I can check in on Tanya, too, when we go to the coast. And I can call Nina.'

'Okay,' I said. 'Do you know where to go?'

'Yes just downtown. There are a bunch of places. Cellphones are big here.'

And, indeed, cellphones were big in Kenya. On the car ride from the hotel to downtown, a ride that took about twenty minutes but only because traffic was so congested, I kept seeing advertisements for Safaricom, Kenya's largest cellphone provider, and a few ads for its much smaller competitors. Instead of us calling Billy Mutinda for a ride, the security guard at the front gate simply opened the gate and signalled for a car to pull in, one of the many that waited outside the gate for a fare.

The sun was bright and high and I was excited to see downtown Nairobi. People walked alongside the idling cars. Black exhaust filled the air around us but the sky above was endless blue.

'Martin told me that the city had passed emission laws, like if your car was emitting black smoke the cops could pull you over,' Boris said. 'But it became just another way for the cops to bribe people, so the law's not really upheld anymore.'

Both of us needed cash so we got dropped off at a bank on Haile Selassie Ave. They had an ATM out front. From there we went to the first cellphone store we saw. Within twenty minutes Boris had us outfitted with simple Nokia phones with 200 international minutes on both phones for approximately seventy-five dollars U.S., so less than forty dollars each. It seemed worth it, and we'd recoup most of our expenses.

We strolled up to Aga Khan Walk and came upon the Nairobi Cinema. I said to Boris, 'I just want to see what's playing.' And I walked up and checked. I ran back and said to Boris, 'The new Bond's playing here, too: *Casino Royale*. Same as home.'

Since we were both thirsty, we stopped at a café for tea and bottled water.

'What's on the itinerary for tonight?' I said.

'There's an opening reception for the festival. But it's just at the hotel's restaurant. So it's easy,' he said.

'Good. I want to try and catch up on some rest.'

'Me too,' said Boris. 'It takes a few days to acclimatize. Really, that's the only problem – we don't have enough time here this trip – by the time you're feeling good and not jetlagged, we pretty much have to go.'

'Yes,' I said. 'But we'll be home in time to celebrate the new year.'

'Nina's having people over, if you want to stop by,' he said.

'Thanks. I'll have to talk to Stacey first.'

We decided to walk back to the hotel alongside Kenyatta Ave. It took us about forty minutes and it was the hottest part of the day, the sun high above us as we walked through exhaust fumes. Nevertheless, we were both happy, Boris especially so. Back in Montreal, I'd never see him smile so much, or for that matter, feel like taking a walk for forty minutes alongside traffic. But here he did, with a smile on his face.

'Those are called *matatus*,' Boris said, pointing at a wildly painted minibus.

His surprisingly sunny disposition kept me from focusing on how generally lousy I was feeling, with the jetlag, worrying about Stacey, and feverishness from the shots. I took in the greens and beiges and reds as we got further away from the downtown core. The foliage thickened the closer we got to the hotel.

We turned onto Milimani Rd. and there was the hotel. I memorized the route we took, in an attempt to orient myself, knowing it wouldn't work.

II

The hotel bar-slash-restaurant was packed with festivalgoers: journalists, painters, musicians, students, poets, novelists, editors, et cetera. I stood with a bottle of water in my hand, wearing a blue sport coat, a black polo, jeans and sneakers, talking to no one, taking in the room. Anita Khalsa, a festival organizer, said a few words, as did Kenyan literary force Kenneth Karega, a brilliant and charismatic writer Boris had introduced me to in Montreal the previous year. Here, in Nairobi, he was a star. And it was clear when I'd met him in Montreal that he'd be a star worldwide within a few years. But both Anita and Kenneth kept their opening greetings brief and the party began. Due to the vodka drinking in Martin's backyard the night before, I decided to abstain from drinking alcohol and to stick to waters. Besides, I needed to rehydrate. I still felt dizzy and generally discombobulated, though I was doing my best to pull it together for the party, and I was enjoying the atmosphere, too. There were people of all ages and from all walks of life. And everybody seemed happy to be at the party, at the festival, and I was happy, too, even though I felt *off*.

'Are you a writer?' a beautiful young woman in a yellow dress asked me and I was taken off guard.

'Sorry?' I said.

'Are you a writer?' she repeated. 'Are you here for the festival?'

'Yes, I'm here writing an article about the festival.'

'Oh, that's nice. Where are you from?'

'I'm from Canada, visiting from Montreal.'

'Montreal!' she said. 'I couldn't handle the snow.' She shivered and it did look funny, with her in a beautiful silky yellow dress, while the hot sun still shone over Nairobi.

'Ha, yes, it's bad,' I said, 'especially this time of year. Are you from here?'

'Yes, I grew up in Nairobi, near Westlands.'

'My name's John,' I said.

'Hana,' she said, extending her hand, which I lightly shook.

'Do you write?' I said.

'Yes, but I'm studying,' she said. 'I attend the University of Nairobi, where I study creative writing and literature. I'm a student of Kenneth's.'

'Oh, that's great,' I said, but then Hana was called away by one of her friends on the other side of the restaurant.

'Excuse me,' she said. 'We'll talk later, John. Nice to meet you.'

'Nice to meet you too, Hana.'

Mark approached me and said quietly, 'She's cute.'

'Extremely,' I said.

'It looked like you liked her.'

'I did. I'm not used to beautiful women approaching me out of nowhere.'

'Who is?' said Mark. He took a sip of the Tusker in his hand and said, 'My buddy from Chicago, Jason, should be here soon. I want you to meet him. He's been living in Kenya for the past year and a half, working with the Peace Corps. We've been friends since we were little kids. He's a great guy. I told him to just show up for the opening.'

'Right on,' I said. 'That's awesome you have an old friend here.'

'Oldest, maybe even.'

'Have you had a chance to say hey to Boris yet?'

'Only for a minute,' said Mark. 'We'll have to hang out more later.'

'When are you reading?' I said.

'I read a couple of times. But I'm teaching one of the poetry workshops the festival's putting on, too, which will be both here and in Lamu. For locals, the workshop's pretty much free. For visitors, it's a little more but still inexpensive. I'm not really getting paid,' he said, 'but all my travel and accommodations are covered and I get a small, a very small, stipend.'

'I doubt I'll break even on this adventure, but it seemed worth it.'

'Definitely,' he said. 'When do you get to travel to Kenya! This is my second time and I'm glad to be back.'

'Other than the jetlag and so on I'm super happy to be here.'

'The jetlag's annoying,' said Mark. 'But it goes away.'

'Also, I'm having a bit of a reaction to my vaccinations or something,' I said. 'My arm's all bruised and I'm pretty out of it, a little off.'

'That'll go away, too,' he said. 'You just need some real rest.'

'That's why I'm drinking water,' I said, slightly holding up my bottle.

'Yes, hydration!' he said and took a sip of Tusker.

Mark started talking to a literature professor from the University of Nairobi and I discreetly made a few notes for the article in a small notebook I had in my pocket. Really, in many ways, the article was Boris's idea, an excuse for us to get to Kenya, and then Nina had insisted that we take their daughter to visit her grandparents, which was fine by all, though before we left Nina had become regretful about her decision to send Tanya, that is to say, to be separated from Tanya, separated for the first time for more than twenty-four hours since Tanya was born eight years ago. Nina warned me: 'John, Boris will wander off or check his email and forget to watch Tanya.' She'd cornered me in their home, backing me up against the wall. 'I'm counting on you to watch her, too,' she said, a finger in my face. 'And if anything happens to Tanya, I'm also holding you responsible.'

She wasn't kidding, I knew that, so I simply nodded.

The magazine back in Canada wasn't giving us much space, so I was basically going to write a gloss of the literary festival and some of its participants. Boris would take beautiful photos of some of the writers and various artists and landscapes. It was an easy gig, though not well paying.

Boris found me and said he'd just talked to the writer from *Esquire*, Elizabeth, at the bar and she was being put up in a luxury vacation home when we hit Lamu, she'd told Boris, though she'd been asked to write a sort of review of said vacation home, as it and homes like it were available year-round for rent with staff, et cetera, to the super wealthy. But she was writing profiles of some of the festival's participants, too. *Esquire* was doing a whole Africa issue, she'd told Boris, and supposedly it was being guest-edited by Bono and The Edge.

'Well, thankfully our piece won't be held to such high editorial scrutiny,' I said.

'No kidding,' said Boris. 'Elizabeth is cool, though.'

'I'm sure,' I said.

Boris said, 'Hey, tomorrow Sveta's going to pick me up around ten-thirty and we're taking Tanya and Alexi to, like, a small nature reserve, with giraffes and monkeys and such things. The kids like it. You're welcome to join us ... '

'Definitely,' I said. 'I'm in.'

'Good. It'll be, well ... it'll be okay,' he said.

'You don't like it?'

'The kids do. You can pet a giraffe. Why do I need to pet a freakin' giraffe!'

'Don't judge me if I pet a giraffe,' I said. 'That'll be hard for me to resist.'

'It's pretty cool to get so close,' he said.

'Boris!' we heard, 'John!' We turned around and saw our friend Stanley – a local poet; journalist for the *Standard*, writing two columns, one under a pseudonym and one under his given name; a TV personality, I was once told; a short-story writer; novelist; and gossip blogger, I was once told, too, though I'm not sure – standing with his arms opened wide to embrace us both, looking dapper in a dark corduroy sport coat and straw hat with a black band.

'Stanley,' said Boris, 'great to see you, man!' and they hugged.

'You're looking good,' I said, and we hugged, too.

'John, Boris, I'm so happy to see you both. I've spent the afternoon writing a piece for deadline and I could really use a refreshment. Perhaps a small beer or a vodka.'

'I had a little too much vodka last night,' I said.

'Oh, yes, what were you doing? You arrived last night?'

'Yes, we got in last night and got a little lit up with Boris's father-in-law.'

'Ha, yes,' said Stanley, 'Martin served some vodka – he's a Russophile like me.'

'Yes, but he speaks Russian and lived in Russia, unlike you,' said Boris. 'After the long flights it probably wasn't the best idea to drink vodka.'

'Well, maybe you should have another vodka, but not too many tonight.'

'I'll pass,' I said. 'For now at least.'

'Me too,' said Boris, 'but please go ahead ... '

'I think I will,' said Stanley.

Stanley, Boris, Mark and his friend Jason, and Stanley's sister, Sharon, and I sat at a table on the terrace. It was dark out now and loud with what I thought to be cicadas, though I wasn't sure if there were cicadas in Nairobi.

The party had thinned out by at least half, but there were still plenty of people hanging out. Although I'd decided to abstain from alcohol earlier, I was now drinking a Pilsner. Everyone else at the table had been drinking for a while, save Boris, who, like me, had only ordered a beer now that we were seated at a table, after being at the party for hours.

Jason, a vaguely familiar-looking young man, about twenty-seven years old, in well-worn shorts and a disintegrating greyish T-shirt, was telling us about going to see Illinois State Senator Barack Obama this past summer in Nairobi. He was travelling the country with his family, Jason told us. 'His father was Luo, from Nyangoma-Kogelo, near Lake Victoria ... So western Kenya, not far from Kisumu,' he said.

'Sharon and I saw him speak, too,' said Stanley. 'It was very moving.'

'He is a rock star here,' said Sharon.

'Yeah, everyone was going nuts,' said Jason. 'The Obamas were mobbed. It was like Gandhi was visiting.'

'It really was,' said Stanley, 'it really was.'

'He took an HIV test to raise awareness,' said Jason.

'Well, there's a good chance he'll run for U.S. presidency and win,' said Boris.

'Let's hope so,' said Mark.

'If he ran in Kenya he'd win,' said Sharon.

'I got a signed copy of his book,' said Jason, digging into his crammed knapsack.

'I've been meaning to read that,' I said.

He produced a trade paperback copy of Senator Obama's *Dreams from My Father*. Jason passed it to me.

Jason — follow your dreams, he'd written, *Barack Obama*, he'd signed.

I looked up and saw Kenneth Karega get up from the table beside ours, where he'd been sitting, chatting with Nigerian novelist Chimamanda Ngozi Adichie. The two hugged goodbye and Kenneth produced a pack of Marlboro Reds from his shorts pockets and a lighter and put a cigarette in his mouth. He pulled a wicker-bottomed chair up to our table. 'How's it going, guys?' he said, lit his cigarette, and fell into his chair. The wicker set to cracking beneath him as he blew out some smoke.

Somehow, eventually, we got on to the topic of open- and closed-casket funerals. Kenneth said, 'Viewing a dead body makes some sense to me, if you want. But putting makeup on a dead body cancels out the whole purpose of looking at a dead body in the first place – i.e., to see it as only an earthly vessel, now uninhabited by a soul, not the person you knew and loved. But to cover the face in makeup – why, so it's life-like? I find that grotesque. The ghost is gone.'

We laughed and conceded that that made some sense.

'The festival's shaping up to look great,' I said. 'Are you planning to hold it every year?'

'That's the idea, but we might skip next year because of the elections.'

'Do you expect problems?' said Mark.

'Not sure,' he said. 'I hope not but you never know.'

'Why would there be problems?' I said.

'It's going to be Mwai Kibaki, the incumbent president, who's Kikuyu, the country's largest tribe,' said Kenneth, 'against Raila Odinga, the non-incumbent, who's Luo, the country's second largest tribe.'

'Who do you think will win?'

'Odinga's got a real shot. But that's a problem for Kibaki. Odinga's the more democratic of the two, to put it mildly,' he said.

Kenneth's cellphone rang and he stood up from the table to take the call. He paced a section of the patio while smoking and talking.

Boris said, 'One day Kenneth will be the president of Kenya.'

'I'd vote for Kenneth,' said Sharon.

'Hear, hear!' said Stanley, laughing, holding up a bottle of Pilsner, and we all clinked drinks.

I wished everyone goodnight, ordered a bottle of water from the bar and headed for my room. Boris left when I did, too, because we were going to the nature reserve with Sveta and the kids in the a.m.

When I got back to the room I brushed my teeth and washed my tired face. I went for my toiletry kit looking for dental floss. I unzipped my kit and it smelled like the inside of a hockey bag, though it turned out to be valerian pills I'd brought as sleep aids; the cap had come off the bottle and the pills were all over the bottom of the kit. I collected them and put them back in the bottle and swallowed back two with some bottled water before getting into bed. I turned on the TV set in the top left-hand corner of my room and *At War with the Army*, with Dean Martin and Jerry Lewis, was on.

Dean sang, 'It's easier to say *I love you* than *tonda wanda hoy comma kalai*. / And wouldn't you rather say *I love you* than *tonda wanda hoy comma kalai*.'

I stretched out on top of the sheets and propped myself up against the wall with a pillow to watch the film.

Later, Jerry Lewis sings the same song as Dean Martin, but in a dress, wearing a blond wig, to a drunken sergeant who's enamoured with Lewis. That's when I fell asleep for an hour or so.

My dreams were vivid and violent. I tossed and turned and awoke covered in sweat. I felt embarrassed over how much I'd sweat in my sleep, even though no one was around to witness it. I drank some water from the bottle on the bedside table. I shut off the TV.

I knew I wouldn't be falling back asleep any time soon, so I took my laptop out of my knapsack and decided to try and work for a while. I opened a new Word doc and typed out my notes from the party, elaborating on a few of them. I didn't have much of an idea of what I'd write for the article yet. Afterward, I worked on another story, a piece of fiction I was writing, for an hour or so, making little progress, though it occupied me for a while. Then I shut the laptop and picked up a book.

I decided to take one more valerian pill and force myself to sleep at least another hour. First, I jerked off; then, I fell asleep.

Sleep only lasted so long, though I remained motionless in bed for as long as possible. Eventually, restlessness got the best of me and I hit the shower. The shower was hot and the washroom steamed up, and there was no real change in the condition of my arm: that is, it was still discoloured and sore.

I shut off the shower and dried myself. I wiped the steam from the mirror. There was something underneath my eye. I examined myself closely. A blood vessel had burst under my right eye, by the looks of it. Under the eye it was now bruised black and looked like the black grease football players and baseball players use to cut down on the glare from the sunlight. I rubbed at it but it wouldn't come off. It wasn't eye black; it was definitely internal.

When I finished dressing I put on sunglasses before heading out for breakfast.

Only one other man sat on the terrace at a nearby table. He had a greying buzz cut and was drinking a large Tusker at nine a.m. He was also smoking a small cigar. He was thick through the neck and shoulders – the first word I thought when I saw him was *mercenary*. He was extremely red, with sun, booze and blood pressure. Also, in a brash British accent, he was extremely rude to Robert, the waiter.

'I need a beer, pronto, and don't take your bloody time like last time,' he said to Robert. 'You hear me?'

Robert said, 'Yessir,' and turned on his heel.

This man turned and looked at me spitefully, while spitting tobacco flecks from his lips. He held my gaze. I was the first to look away, even though I was wearing sunglasses and he wasn't; still, I flinched first, avoiding the menacing fixity of his gaze.

When he seemed satisfied that I was too weak to bother about, he returned his attention to his beer and cigar. I finished my tea and got up, leaving most of my breakfast, the same breakfast as the day before, untouched. The man paid me no mind when I got up to leave.

In the lobby I bumped into Boris, who was on his way to breakfast.

'Hey man,' I said. 'I'm just going to go to my room to take my pills but I'll be back down soon.'

Sveta picked us up in a hatchback similar to Martin's, with Alexi and Tanya sitting in the backseat. I got in the back with them and Boris rode up front with Sveta. We were going to the Nairobi Animal Orphanage, Sveta told me, when I asked.

'It's not very big,' she said. 'But there are monkeys and giraffes and I've seen lions there before, too, but I'm not sure if there are any there at the moment.'

'Cool,' I said.

'You can feed giraffes,' Sveta said.

'Boris was telling me.'

'I'm going to feed a giraffe,' said Tanya. 'I have before but I'm going to again.'

'I think I'll feed a giraffe, too,' I said.

'You should,' said Tanya. 'It's free!'

'Well, with admission,' said Boris.

The drive took approximately half an hour. The park looked somewhat run-down but I spotted several giraffes right away and was surprised by how excited I was to see them. Tanya and Alexi were excited, too, but Sveta and Boris seemed unimpressed. We pulled up to a gate with a guard and Boris paid, then we parked. We got out and instinctively started walking toward an area where one could feed the giraffes on the other side of a fence, by a gigantic tree – an oak tree, I thought, though I had no idea if oak trees grew on the outskirts of Nairobi.

'How much do I owe you?' I said to Boris, as we walked toward the park.

'Nothing, man. I just paid for a car full of people so it's not a big deal,' he said. 'The petting zoo's on me!'

'Ha, well, thanks.'

We walked past a small chain-link fenced-off area, a chain-link cage really, where a solitary ratty hyena drank water from a large brown plastic bowl with the jagged indentations of teethmarks all over it.

By the large tree, there was a handful of people, four or five, with their hands extended, feeding the four giraffes. The giraffes bent their long beautiful necks and ate some form of vegetable pellets right out of the tourists' hands. Small tusked warthogs ran around at the feet of the giraffes.

There was a large sort of gumball machine that dispensed the pellets, without having to put coins in it, and right beside it was an industrial hand-sanitizing station.

Sveta cranked out some feed for the kids and then I cranked out some for myself. Boris picked Tanya up so she could feed a giraffe, who obediently lowered its neck and lapped up the feed, its inky-black eyes big and shiny and dreamy, amber at the edges, with long lashes and heavy lids. The eyes were mesmerizing in their beauty and sublime docility, I thought. An evolved species.

When its tongue emerged, we all laughed uncontrollably, even Boris.

Next, Sveta lifted Alexi up to feed our friend and I patiently awaited my turn. The little boy smiled when the giraffe took the feed but quickly seemed to lose interest, which pleased me, because it meant it was my turn.

I extended my arm and hand, with the pellets held upward, and the giraffe slowly and fluidly shifted its neck and head toward me, briefly acknowledging me with an all-consuming benevolent gaze, then the giant tongue emerged and lapped up the feed. Its long tongue was black at the tip, like hard plastic, though turned a deep purple and then pinkish and moist the further back it went. I laughed like a fool, a fool drunkenly in love, for a moment forgetting my worries, forgetting myself.

Boris and Sveta both smiled at me. I promptly made my way to the hand-sanitizing station.

Sveta watched the kids as they ran around the large tree and Boris and I sat in wooden chairs by a fire pit with no fire, drinking bottled water.

'We'll head back soon,' said Boris, 'so we can change before the reading at the Alliance Française.'

'That's at five?' I said.

'Yes, but we'll leave around fourish. There are shuttle buses leaving from the hotel.'

'All right,' I said. 'It should be good.'

'Yes and it'll be a good place to take some photos for the article,' he said. 'I should've gotten one of you feeding the giraffe.'

'It's probably best the moment's forever effaced,' I said. 'I had a moment of existential revelation and angst while feeding the giraffe: I was convinced of its existence, though unsure of mine.'

'Yes, giant mammals will do that to you,' he said.

Sveta was in the distance talking to an employee of the animal orphanage. She walked to the fire pit with the children and said, 'There're no lions. One's sick and away, the other died.'

We took a different, circuitous route to the car and walked past another cage. Two monkeys sat on top of some rusty chain-link fencing, crudely layered to make a jungle gym.

Back at the hotel Boris and I split up in the lobby, agreeing to meet back downstairs in forty-five minutes. There were people everywhere but I ignored the crowd and returned to the quiet of my room. I would've loved to have lain down for an hour but there wasn't time. I figured I could get away with lying down for fifteen minutes or so, however, so that's what I did.

I put in my small white earphones, from my new iPod Mini, a recent birthday/Christmas gift from Stacey, my girl-friend. When she gave it to me, I was shocked and touched. The gift was expensive – more expensive than either of us could reasonably afford – and we'd been growing apart. When I opened the wrapping paper and saw the gift, it was obvious I was surprised.

'See,' she said, 'I love you very much.'

'You got me an iPod.'

'I got you an iPod.'

I lay on the bed, with my eyes closed, listening to the first twenty minutes of Miles Davis's *In a Silent Way*, then I got up to take another quick shower.

Down in the lobby, festivalgoers waited around for the shuttle buses. Eventually, three mid-sized buses showed up, very modern, air-conditioned, et cetera. I sat beside a poet, Caroline, from Massachusetts, who was writing a collection about Robert Oppenheimer. She'd recently won a prize for her work, she told me.

Caroline was very nice and we talked about Oppenheimer while we drove the ten minutes or so to the Alliance Française. But then Céline Dion's 'My Heart Will Go On' came on the bus's stereo and it really hit me how internationally famous Dion in fact was; in Quebec, I took it for granted Céline's music played from the clouds but I didn't expect to hear her in Nairobi. 'I love this song,' said Caroline. 'My mom and I belt it out together!'

The reading was out back, in a large beautiful sunlit courtyard. It was bright and I was glad to be wearing sunglasses. There was a stage at the back of the courtyard, with large leafy plants on either side of a podium, and a DJ spinning records while people milled about, sipping on drinks.

I bumped into Stanley at the bar, which was just inside the building, though the back was open-air, so you could still see the stage from the bar.

'You're drinking red wine,' I said, while he sipped from a plastic-stemmed cup.

'The wine's free,' he said.

'Wine it is,' I said, and picked up a pre-poured cup from the bar.

There were some introductory remarks given by Kenneth's sister, May, who emceed the event, welcoming everyone, thanking the Alliance Française for hosting the event, and then the readings began. Stanley and I stood at the back but could see and hear everything; I took some notes.

The first reader was Doreen Baingana, a writer from Uganda, now studying in the U.S., who read a story from her collection, *Tropical Fish*, which had recently won the Commonwealth Writers' Prize. The reading was excellent and moving and Stanley said, 'You should read her book. It's really very good.'

'I'll pick it up.'

The next quote-unquote reader was a truly dreadful spoken-word poet whose name I never bothered to write down. It was simply a bunch of shouting, et cetera, and strangely juvenile anti-Americanism; even though none of us were fans of the Bush administration, it was clear she was painting with a broad, sloppy brush. A few times, she punched her chest like Céline Dion, without the gifted voice.

While waiting out the spoken-word poet, who was onstage far longer than the first reader, Stanley took the opportunity to refresh our wine.

After the poet had mercifully stopped shouting and left the stage, Chimamanda Adichie read from her new novel, *Half of a Yellow Sun*, and she was wonderful.

'That was great,' I said to Stanley, when she'd finished.

'Chima's incredible,' he said. 'Did you read *Purple Hibiscus*?'

'I did,' I said. 'I liked it a lot. Kenneth told me to read it.'

'It's a wonderful novel,' he said. 'Coetzee blurbed it!'

People ambled around the courtyard talking, drinking, laughing, while two young women set up some of their musical gear. One of them, DJ Flora, got behind the turntables and started spinning some records, and then she introduced MC Karen, a long-legged young woman in black jean short-shorts and a black crop-top, worn brown leather boots with a small heel, and close-cropped hair. Her almond-shaped eyes were large and both smoky and shining, her smile radiant, as she demanded the crowd's attention. The large group, too, stopped all conversation to watch DJ Flora and MC Karen.

Like a prizefighter, MC Karen belted out her rhymes, in English and Kiswahili, from what I could tell, singing, too, beautifully, between her hard-hitting raps. Her confidence was astounding, and she mesmerized the courtyard full of people.

'This is amazing,' I said to Stanley, 'like, truly amazing!'

'MC Karen and DJ Flora are terrific.'

'You know them?'

'A little,' he said. 'They play around. They're playing at the party after at Club Afrique.'

'The music's so good,' I said. 'They're – wow!'

'*Moto Kama Pasi*,' he said. 'Hot as passports ... '

DJ Flora and MC Karen only played three songs and then the music stopped, but people hung around for another hour before we went to the nightclub. The sun had started to set, but I kept my sunglasses on, as I felt extremely sensitive to the light. Stanley went off to talk to some friends and I hit the books table to pick up some things.

Two young people manned the table: a young man and a young woman, both enthusiastic.

I bought a green-and-yellow hardcover copy of Chimamanda Adichie's new novel, *Half of a Yellow Sun*, a Kenyan edition, and I also bought a hardcover copy of Doreen Baingana's *Tropical Fish*. The young woman at the books table gave me a complimentary copy of an anthology of East African short fiction and a tote bag for buying two hardcovers.

The nightclub was close by on Museum Hill, but it still took a while to get there because travelling on a shuttle with people is slow no matter what. We sat in the parking lot for approximately twenty minutes to drive five minutes. But I wasn't complaining. We were all high on the music we'd just heard. It's what everyone was talking about while we waited for the bus to fill up and on the short ride.

The bus pulled up to the club and we waited while a man opened a gate. We disembarked and lined up and were given tickets to present to a doorman down a hallway before entering the large nightclub.

The large room looked almost empty, though there were people there, many in fact, but the room was so big that it still appeared almost empty, and a band played on the stage: guitar, bass, drums, keyboards, a few horns, several singers, dancing and singing, women and men. There were very few people on the huge dance floor. But we were a large group, so the club started to feel a little fuller.

There were several bars – one on each side of the dance floor and a small bar in the back, a VIP lounge – so I sat on a stool at the bar to the left of the entrance and waited for a bartender. I saw they had Heineken and ordered one from the bartender, after he served the many women waiting first. I was relieved to not be drinking Pilsner. Although I enjoyed the beer, my stomach felt tender. Heineken seemed like a safer bet, even though it was a bit pricier.

Mark and Jason sat down on stools with me and ordered Pilsners.

'Jason's going to come to Lamu with us,' said Mark.

'Right on,' I said.

'It's my favourite place on earth,' said Jason. 'You'll love it, so laid-back, no cars, donkeys, beaches, *dhows* ... Ah, it's the best.'

Jason seemed so familiar in his instant likeability – charming, funny and kind.

'The second I get there I put on a *kikoy*,' he said, 'and that's that.'

'What's that?' I said.

'It's like a wrap,' said Mark, 'a sort of beach wrap.'

'But much nicer,' said Jason. 'They're Swahili *kikoys* and they're rectangular loom-woven cloth and very colourful with different, beautiful patterns and they can be used for anything: a beach towel, for a baby,' he said, miming a baby wrapped in the garment, tied around his neck and held in his arms. 'People use them as turbans and tablecloths and curtains, headscarves, wraparound skirts.'

'They're pretty cool,' said Mark.

'And they're 100 percent cotton and dry very fast.'

'I'll definitely get one,' I said.

'I mean, you can get one here in the markets, but they'll be better and cheaper in Lamu. I can't wait to lose the jeans and put one on.'

I felt a buzz in my pocket and patted myself down, finding my Nokia; it was my first text from Boris, the only person who had my number: *Man b there soon u ok*. So I wrote back, *All good at club c u soon*.

The dance floor began to fill up, a lightshow spinning on the stage and on the floor.

Jason said, 'Lamu's pretty much dry, though, on account of it being a predominantly Muslim island, so we should stock up before we fly out.'

'Good idea,' said Mark.

'We'll hit a Nakumatt downtown,' said Jason. 'It's a supermarket chain.'

My tongue kept digging into the side of my cheek, where I felt a canker sore. I swigged some beer to distract my tongue.

'I have to hit the loo,' said Jason, and he stood up from his stool.

Mark and I watched the dance floor, the beautiful women, the dizzying lightshow, the smiling faces, and Mark said, 'This is pretty sweet, right?'

'It is,' I said, and we clinked bottles.

'It's so good to see Jason,' he said. 'It's been years but we went to elementary school together and high school. He's always been such a good friend. But I haven't seen him since he joined the Peace Corps and moved here.'

'He's a great guy,' I said. 'That's clear right away, for sure.'

'And really funny,' said Mark.

'He seems so familiar. I feel like I've known him a long time. His face. His smile. His intonation. It all seems really familiar. He reminds me of a buddy back home, I think, but I can't remember which buddy,' I said.

'He reminds you of Nathan Lane.'

'What?' I said. 'The actor?'

'Yes,' said Mark, 'the actor.'

'I guess he kind of does,' I said, smiling, Mark smiling back at me, watching my recognition kick in.

'He's Nathan Lane's second cousin.'

'No shit!' I said. 'Oh man! That makes so much sense.'

'He looks like him, right?'

'He looks like his younger brother,' I said. 'And he sounds like him, too!'

'Funny, right?'

'That's incredible,' I said. 'No wonder he's so damn likeable.'

'I know,' said Mark.

'That's crazy,' I said.

'He acts, too – was in all the plays in our schools and throughout university, too, but he was having a tough time getting parts and then came here.'

'Man, I'd cast him in everything,' I said.

'Me too,' said Mark. 'He'll get back at it. He's just taking a break. In high school he did one hell of a Nathan Detroit. People still talk about it.'

'Does Nathan Lane know he's an actor?'

'I think so,' said Mark. 'But he doesn't want to call in any favours or anything, though he says Nathan Lane's super nice.'

'Is Jason's last name Lane?'

'No. DeMarco. His dad's Italian.'

'Is he sensitive about being Nathan Lane's cousin or is it something that comes up?'

'Oh it comes up. You can ask him about it sometime. Hey, what happened to your eye?' he said. 'It looks like you burst a blood vessel.'

'I think that's what happened. Probably all the travel. Does it look bad?'

'No, just a little bruised. You can barely see it in this light.'

Boris walked in the club, looking a little frenzied, and spotted me right away; he joined us.

'What happened to you?' I said.

Boris said, 'I got caught up in a conversation with the director of the Alliance Française and missed the bus. He dropped me off, though.'

'Good.'

'Yeah but then I just spent the last few minutes explaining to the doorman why I didn't have a ticket and wasn't going to pay,' he said.

'Is everything all right?' said Mark.

'Everything's fine. It just took a minute to explain.'

'Do you want a beer?' said Mark.

'Sure,' he said.

Jason returned from the washroom and now the resemblance to Nathan Lane was unignorable but I did my best not to bring it up. Still, I was burning to tell Boris.

Mark passed Boris a Pilsner and we watched the stage, where MC Karen and DJ Flora were setting up.

Boris said, 'Did you see these young women?'

'Yes,' I said. 'Amazing, right.'

'I couldn't believe it,' he said. 'Really powerful stuff.'

And again, MC Karen dominated the room. Tough but welcoming, angry yet kind. The mix of languages worked wonderfully and seemed natural, fluid, musical. Everyone in the large club watched the stage – the people danced facing the stage, watching the show, dancing with MC Karen.

Between songs, Boris said, 'This is a room full of artists and writers and everyone's jaws drop when these two play. Incredible.'

After the short set I ordered a bottle of water. A redheaded woman sitting on a barstool beside me said, 'Smart move.'

'Sorry?' I said.

'The water. Smart move. It's a good idea to stay hydrated,' she said, as she sipped her white wine.

'I had some wine at the reading,' I said, 'only two small glasses and a beer. But I thought I should have a water.'

'Yeah, I try not to drink hard liquor at all.'

'Oh yeah. Any specific reason?'

'*Reasons*,' she said. 'I turn into a different person.'

'I get that,' I said.

'No, like quite literally, I turn into a different person.'

'Who?'

'Kitten Mather.'

'Kitten Mather.'

'Kitten Mather,' she said. 'And she's nuts and a pain in the ass.'

'Oh wow. What does she do?'

'She breaks things, she doesn't stop partying, and she sleeps around,' she said. 'I don't want to get into trouble here or hurt myself.'

'Yeah, of course, makes sense.'

'Last time I turned into Kitten Mather, after drinking champagne and vodka at this restaurant in Miami called BED, where you eat in a bed, I went down on my friend, who was there with a guy.'

'Oh shit,' I said.

'Yeah.'

'At BED?'

'At BED, in the bed, mortifying,' she said.

'Oh my god.'

'Yeah.'

'Who were you with?' I said.

'Some Japanese businessmen.'

'Really,' I said. 'How did that come about?'

'It's a super expensive fancy restaurant and my girlfriend – '

'The girl you went down on.'

'Exactly. She, Julia, knew this guy from Japan who's a friend of her boss and he was in Miami on business and so she asked me if I'd be his friend's date. I said sure. It was fun, like, till I lost my mind. I mean, it was still fun, too much fun, but I wasn't in control at all.'

'That's amazing,' I said. 'And frightening, too.'

'Yeah. It's wild. My twenty-ninth birthday was even worse. Anyway, now I just stick to wine or beer,' she said, holding her wineglass by the stem.

'So Kitten Mather's your alter ego, but what's your civilian name?'

'Melissa,' she said, extending her hand.

'Nice to meet you, Melissa,' I said. 'I'm John.'

'What's your deal?'

'I'm here for the festival. I'm writing an article about it and East African lit, et cetera, in general. Why are you here?'

'For the festival. I'm taking some of the workshops, a poetry one.'

'Oh, my buddy Mark's teaching that.'

'Yeah. I'm just finishing my MFA in North Carolina.'

'That's great.'

'I'm glad I came. You here alone?'

'I travelled with my friend Boris, a photographer, and his daughter. His in-laws live here.'

'You didn't come with a girlfriend?'

'No, but I have a girlfriend back home. Stacey,' I said. 'That's her name.'

'Stacey,' said Melissa. 'Well, cheers.' She bumped her wineglass up against my bottle of water. 'We need to get you a drink,' said Melissa.

I drank a Heineken with Melissa from North Carolina, who was quite funny, if not a little intense, and then checked in with Boris, who sat with Stanley and some others at the bar.

'That MC Karen and Flora are sensational,' he said. 'We need to find out if they have a CD.'

'Good idea,' I said. 'They're phenomenal. Really, the best live music I've seen in a long time.'

'Agreed,' said Boris. 'Tomorrow there's a group going to the Rift Valley for Maasai barbecue. A friend of Martin's, a guy he grew up with, has a place, a restaurant sort of, and we've arranged for a small shuttle to take a bunch of us. We'll be eating a lot of meat, I imagine.'

'What time are we leaving?'

'Around noon. It's about an hour or so out of the city, on the road to Nakuru, basically, and we'll be gone a bit.

'Sounds like fun,' I said, and a little down the bar I spotted MC Karen on her own, waiting to order a drink. 'Hey, man, I'm going to ask MC Karen if she has any CDs. Do you think I should?'

'Definitely,' he said. 'Say hello – find out about the CDs!'

I felt somewhat foolish but I'd been drinking so also felt a little brave. Besides, my intention was to tell her how much I enjoyed her music. Standing beside her at the bar I said: 'I loved your shows, both here and at the Alliance Française. You and DJ Flora are great.'

'*Asante sana*,' she said, offering her hand. 'Karen.'

'John,' I said, holding her hand. She didn't have a drink yet so I said, 'Can I get you a drink? I need another beer, anyway.'

'Sure,' she said and smiled. 'I'll have a beer. Thanks, John.'

I ordered two Heinekens and asked her if she had an album.

'Not yet,' she said. 'We're recording now. Tonight, even – after this beer I need to get going to our studio in Westlands.

'Oh, right on. Are you far along, like almost done?'

'We have a few more tracks to do but it's getting close,' she said.

She asked where I was from and what I was doing in Nairobi and I told her I'm a writer and a journalist covering the festival for a magazine in Canada, writing about East African artists.

'You should come to our studio,' she said. 'We'll have these beers and then go. Do you play any instruments?'

'I play guitar.'

'Perfect. We need bass and six-string, anything!'

'That sounds like fun but I think I'm expected to stick around here tonight.'

'Well, can you come tomorrow night? We're recording late tomorrow, like nine or ten, but we'll see. We share the space with a bunch of other musicians.'

'Yeah, I'd do tomorrow night. Sure.'

'Do you have a phone?'

'I do!' I said.

'Give it to me,' she said, and I complied and she typed her number into it, texted herself, and she said, 'I'll sms you.'

A new band started playing and Karen said, 'I love this song,' and pulled me down onto the dance floor. She danced wonderfully, naturally, and I stood awkwardly on the floor holding my beer bottle. The writer from *Esquire*, Elizabeth, was dancing beside us with her husband and it looked like they'd taken lessons from Uma Thurman and John Travolta's choreographer for *Pulp Fiction*. This increased my self-consciousness with respect to my bad dancing. I put the bottle down on the side of the dance floor. MC Karen laughed and took my hands and we danced.

MC Karen left with DJ Flora for their studio and I sat back with Boris, silent, fantasizing about spending time with MC Karen. I thought about dancing with her, even though I'm not a good dancer. I thought about playing on her tracks, discovering her Nairobi, basking in the light of her beauty, confidence and virtuosic talent.

My reverie was interrupted by Kenneth, who was with a tall slim man who had a slim moustache, and he said, 'Guys, I want you to meet my friend Richard Onyango. One of the greatest painters to come out of Kenya.' The slim man stood smiling, and Kenneth continued, 'Richard, this is Boris, the Russian photographer I was telling you about, and John, a very good writer from Canada.'

'It's an honour to meet you two,' said Richard Onyango. 'It's an honour to meet fellow artists.'

The band stopped playing and Kenneth took the stage. He thanked everyone for coming, for being part of the festival, for celebrating African art, specifically East African art, and in the spirit of celebrating art, he said, he wanted to introduce all of us to a very special artist, in fact, one of the best, a true original, Richard Onyango. I took out my small notebook and pen. Onyango stood beside Kenneth – Onyango smiling, tall, hair pomaded, in a silky shirt, a leather jacket, a silver-studded belt, tight jeans and pointy silver-toed black-and-grey crocodile-skin boots. 'Onyango's story is quite miraculous,' said Kenneth, 'the story of an artist finding his form, or forms, and his muse, or muses, rather. But I'll let him tell you his story,' said Kenneth, 'a short version of a remarkable life.'

Kenneth and Richard exchanged smiles and Richard slowly came to the microphone, smiling benevolently, looking super-cool. 'Thank you all,' he said, 'thank you very much,' as we applauded, the whole nightclub, though we were all bewildered, too, for this wasn't what anyone was expecting, especially late into the evening, after several hours of music, dancing and drinks. 'I'm very honoured to be with so many artists,' said Richard, 'from all over the world – Boris and John,' he said, pointing at us, 'and Ed,' he said, pointing at a poet standing near us. Boris and I laughed, surprised he mentioned us from the stage, in front of so many people, when he'd met us only minutes before. 'And thank you, Kenneth,' said Richard, 'for this festival.' Kenneth smiled from side-stage. 'I was a drummer,' said Richard, 'a drummer playing in Mombasa, at a hotel, a very nice hotel,' he said, 'and people would come from all over the world to visit Mombasa, and to drink and dance at the hotel.' Richard slowly walked to the side of the stage and produced a portfolio and walked back to the microphone. He produced a print of a painting of himself drumming, with a band, but from behind the kit, behind himself, an action painting, his arms in motion, drumsticks in the air. 'One night I saw a blond woman enjoying the music, enjoying the music very much, with her friends, and she was very, very fat,' he said, 'and very, very beautiful.' He lowered the painting he was holding back into the portfolio. 'Her arms were thick, her waist like an hourglass, and her buttocks were big, very big,' said Richard, 'and she was very, very beautiful. We played and at the end of the night she tipped me a hundred shillings, which was a lot, at the time,' said Richard, 'and more than anyone else in the band got. I thought about her all the time,' said Richard, 'and a few weeks later, I was playing in a nightclub, playing my drum set, when I saw the fat woman again, sitting on her own this time, and I was very excited to see her. After the set she bought me a drink and I went to thank her,' he said, 'and when I talked to her, my heartbeat went rapid, for she was very beautiful, the most beautiful woman I had seen. My name is Richard, I told her,' he told us, 'and my name is Drosie, she said back. Drosie found me playing in the night-club and it surprised me greatly,' he said, 'but I was delighted. I grew up in Kisii, Kenya, and even as a child I made pictures, instead of taking photographs,' and he made like he was snapping a picture. 'When I saw the Mitsubishi trucks I'd draw them,' he said, and produced from his portfolio a print of a painting of a large Mitsubishi truck, a lorry, on a dusty high-way, 'and I'd drum always, too,' he said. 'Drosie took me into her life,' he said, 'and she was very rich and I lived with Dr. Souzy Drosie as her husband.' He produced a print of a large woman, Drosie, sitting at a table with a glass of wine, her shoes off and to the side of her naked feet, her bosom ample and her gaze like a lioness's. The painting was erotic, in a way, and certainly compelling; he then produced a print of Drosie nude, only wearing bikini-style underwear, her breasts free, her foot on an ottoman or small upholstered stool. Richard smiled out at the crowd, radiating a strange kind of light. 'I grew to love Drosie very much,' he said, and he produced a print of her kissing him against a Mercedes-Benz outside a nightclub, her largeness pressing him tight against the car. 'We were lovers,' he said, 'and I lived as her husband,' he said, 'but Drosie was very jealous. I was no longer allowed to play music with my friends,' he said, 'because of the other women who came to the shows. But I didn't want other women, I told her, and I didn't want young girls,' he said. 'I liked that Drosie was older than me,' he said, 'older and wiser. But, as I said, I missed my drums, so one weekend I devised a lie so I could go play drums, saying I was seeing family, but Drosie suspected I wanted to play in nightclubs. So she went looking for me,' he said, 'and she found me and at the end of the set, she pulled me from behind my drum set.' He produced a print of Drosie pulling him from behind the kit. 'She was very mad at me,' he said, 'but we went home. Then,' he said, 'I started having nightmares about Drosie. I had premonitions,' he said, 'that she would soon die. I had dreams that angels were trying to take her from me,' he said, 'and I held on to her legs, not letting the angels take her away, and we were both wearing only light clothes. I woke Drosie from her pleas-ant sleep with sweating and shaking and screaming,' he said. He produced a print of an angel flying high in the sky, carry-ing Drosie, as he held on to the unravelling fabric she wore. 'Later,' he said, 'she went off driving her Mercedes-Benz and collapsed and the car drifted to the side of the road. She was taken to hospital,' he said, 'and I arrived and she died.' He produced a print of a painting of Drosie in a hospital bed, doctors around her, life having left her. 'I wept bitterly,' said Richard, 'and the doctors told me she died of bad blood pressure and a heart attack. The clock in this painting says six o'clock,' said Richard, pointing to a clock on the hospital room wall in the painting, 'which is the time she died,' he said. 'Drosie changed my life and I will love her forever,' he said. 'And when I became an artist, now I paint my life with Drosie and often paint other very fat women, very fat beautiful women.' He smiled out at the crowd. 'Thank you for having me here, I'm very grateful, thank you very much,' he said, and we all applauded and Kenneth took the microphone.

'Richard Onyango, everybody,' said Kenneth, 'and prints of his paintings will be for sale in the lobby at the Heron

Court Hotel tomorrow afternoon, and Richard will be there to sign them, too. Another round of applause for Richard,' said Kenneth.

'That was very strange,' I said to Boris.

'Yes, indeed, very strange,' he said.

'But the paintings are strangely sublime.'

'Amazing,' said Boris. 'I just don't think anyone was expecting that at a discotheque.'

We laughed.

'That guy might be the coolest man I've ever seen,' I said.

'Perhaps,' said Boris. 'He might be.'

'If the prints aren't overly expensive I'm going to buy a couple,' I said.

'Me too!' he said.

Kenneth invited Boris and me to the VIP lounge, where a group of people were drinking and a DJ was spinning records.

'I want to introduce you guys to my father,' said Kenneth, and he brought us over to a handsome old gentleman sitting on a sofa with Kenneth's sister and some others.

'*Baba*,' said Kenneth, 'these are my friends Boris and John.' He turned to us. 'Guys,' he said proudly, 'this is my father, Ezekiel.'

We shook hands and it was clear Ezekiel's eyesight was failing him, his corneas cloudy, his face kind. He seemed happy, handsome, purblind and smiling, his hands on his knees, his back straight, surrounded by family and friends.

Things were winding down and Billy Ocean's 'Get Outta My Dreams, Get into My Car' played and Stanley sang along, dancing, and we all laughed. His sister Sharon popped her shoulders along to the song, smiling, and I was happy, too.

A bunch of people were heading to a club called Florida 2000, but I'd had enough to drink and was beat. Boris and I got on one of the shuttle buses back to the hotel.

Back in my room, I felt I was getting soft so I got down on the floor and did some push-ups and sit-ups. While doing some sit-ups, I heard a knock at the door and I wondered whether I was making too much noise. I opened the door and it was Melissa from North Carolina, from the bar.

'Hey,' she said and walked into my room.

'Hey,' I said. 'What's going on?'

'I thought maybe you want to hang out,' she said, pressing up against me. And she kissed me. And I kissed her back.

'What do you think your girlfriend would say?' she said. 'What would Stacey say?' she whispered in my ear.

'All right, sorry,' I said. 'You have to go.' And I opened the door to the room. She walked out. 'Goodnight,' I said. 'And thanks for stopping by.'

'Goodnight,' she said and smiled, a bit devilishly, though also warmly, so I smiled back.

I closed the door and did some push-ups, hoping they'd rid me of my guilt. I was glad things didn't develop, though, so I kept doing push-ups.

Eventually, I got into bed. I closed my eyes. I fell asleep.

In the morning I ate only tea and toast, so as not to ruin my appetite, but I wanted to have something in my stomach before taking my pills. I finally felt somewhat rested, even though we were out late, but I'd slept a bit at least, a few hours, like four or five – the most I'd slept since landing in Nairobi.

My eye looked a little better, too, the bruising underneath fading.

I bumped into Mark at breakfast and he said, 'I was just talking to Elizabeth, the *Esquire* writer, and she isn't doing so well.'

'What's wrong?' I said.

'I guess after the club last night a bunch of them went back to Kenneth's sister's place and they were all boozing, but Elizabeth decided to stop drinking and instead drank water from May's Brita and today she's having GI issues.'

'Oh man, that's terrible.'

'Yeah, not pleasant.'

'I have some pills the doctor gave me at the Tropical Diseases Clinic in Montreal, like basically a double dose of Imodium with an antibiotic, too. He only gave me a few,' I said, 'because I gather they're pretty potent and will block you up for like a month if you overdo it. I'll give her a couple.'

'I'm sure she'd appreciate it,' said Mark.

After breakfast, after returning to my room to take the antimalarials and grab the stomach meds, while waiting for our bus, I spotted Elizabeth in the lobby and walked over to her and said, 'Hey, I heard you aren't feeling well, like having stomach issues.'

She said, 'You could hear me from your room?'

'Ha, no,' I said. 'But Mark told me you were having some GI issues, from drinking from May's Brita.'

'I feel like I'm dying,' she said, rubbing her stomach.

'Well I've got some pills, some Ciprofloxacin, for bacterial infections.' We looked at each other. 'It'll help your stomach,' I said. 'I got the pills from the Tropical Diseases Clinic in Montreal, before the trip.'

I produced two large pills from my pocket.

'Here,' I said. 'Take these.'

She accepted.

'Thank you.'

'He only gave me four, said they're powerful.'

'Excellent!' Elizabeth said. 'I'll try anything. Thanks again.'

On our way out of the city we drove past Kibera, one of the largest slums on the planet, both retrograde and futuristic, off in the distance. Boris had visited once and taken some stunning photos but that's the closest I'd get.

The bus stopped once, so people could pee if they had to and I did so I did. I got off the bus and looked down onto the endless valleys and urinated in the shade of thorny acacia branches.

A Maasai, not a herdsman but a herdboy, stood on the side of a hill, wrapped in a reddish *shuka*, a long straight stick in hand and a small skinny calf at his side, negotiating the rocky hillside. Our shuttle bus wound its way up and around the hills. The landscape was crushingly beautiful. My ears popped with the elevation. Most of the green hills were more beige and red than green, the grass patchy and sunburnt.

We arrived at the restaurant, which was outdoors in a Maasai village, though for tourists. Everywhere there were Maasai men in red *shuka*s and covered in colourful beaded jewellery, the beadwork stunning and intricately patterned.

We sat at picnic tables on a patio precipice overlooking the deep, infinite valleys. I saw a young man with a goat on a rope.

Boris said, 'That's our lunch.'

We drank beer and bottled water and took in all the wonder. The air was fresh and I kept closing my eyes under my sunglasses, breathing, meditative.

Although I'd been feeling generally lousy, the beauty of the Rift Valley overwhelmed me. The endless blue sky, the perfect rippling cloudbanks, low down, casting shadows on the valleys, the greens, reds and browns. I'd never seen such perfect sky – the cradle of civilization, without a doubt.

Our lunch arrived on wooden cutting boards.

Basically, it was piles of fresh goat meat, with little piles of salt on the corners of the cutting boards, so as to rub on the meat. We rubbed salt on the goat and ate with our hands. We also ate *ugali*, a doughy cornmeal starch dish, and collard greens.

Kenneth, Boris, Stanley and Sharon all sat at the same picnic table as me, as did a few other people I didn't know. I felt grateful for my friends, for the food, the goat that gave its life, the salts at the corners of the cutting board, the beer and water I drank, for all the love under heaven.

At the end of the meal, a blood sausage called *mūtura* was served.

Kenneth said, 'Most *wazungu* don't like *mūtura*. It's a little intense for them.'

'It's not for me,' said Boris, a sentiment echoed by pretty much everyone at the table, as we stared at the pile of extremely bloody stuffed intestines.

Kenneth ate a morsel and said, 'Delicious!'

I took up the challenge and ate some, too, and blood exploded in my mouth.

'It's good. Bloody,' I said, and everyone laughed. I swigged back some beer.

On the bus ride back from the Rift Valley, I received a text from MC Karen, asking me if I'd be available to meet around six. The cultural attaché of the Embassy of the United States of America, Aruna Jayaraman, had invited a group of us, with embossed invitations, to his home for a literary soireé, 'Spreading the Words,' to be given by some of the visiting American writers, for six-thirty p.m.

But we were flying out for Lamu the next afternoon and the prospect of hanging with MC Karen interested me more than another reading, so I texted Karen back saying I'd love to go to her studio. She wrote saying she'd pick me up in a car at the hotel at six and I said I'd be out front.

I told Boris I'd be skipping the event at the cultural attaché's so as to hang out with MC Karen and he said, 'Man, good choice.'

III

I paced out front of the hotel waiting for MC Karen. I was nervous and wasn't quite sure what to expect. Jason gave me his cell number, if for some reason I got lost or something. My abdomen hurt a little, a soreness incommensurate with the few sit-ups I'd done. The bus to the cultural attaché's house left at five-thirty. Only a small group had been invited. MC Karen was late, like half an hour late, so I went to the restaurant and ordered a bottle of water and watched for her from the terrace.

She showed up a little after seven. I went to greet her and she emerged from the backseat of the car looking gorgeous, again in short-shorts and smiling, with her arms open to greet me, and I no longer cared about her lateness.

A few festivalgoers saw me get in the backseat of the car with MC Karen and I felt good; I felt excited.

'I thought we'd have a beer or two,' she said, 'and meet up with Flora before we hit the studio.'

'I'm game,' I said.

We sat in the backseat, both facing forward, both smiling widely. The sun was bright but starting to set.

The car ride to Westlands took about twenty minutes and we got dropped off at a multi-floored plaza. I paid the driver. Inside, it seemed nearly abandoned, a small abandoned mall. We walked up a few flights of stairs to a food court, an abandoned food court, though one concession remained open, a small bar, with a limited selection: beer, wine coolers or Kenya Cane.

About a half dozen people sat on and around the food court tables. Flora saw us and greeted us right away.

We went up to the bar and I ordered a Tusker and MC Karen ordered the same and Flora opted for a wine cooler. I paid the bartender, who, other than being behind the bar, gave no indication of being a bartender. After he served us, he went and smoked and drank with people at another table.

I sat with the two women and they looked at me and smiled and chatted amongst themselves a little. Occasionally, I'd feel the eyes of others staring at me from nearby tables but I chose to ignore them; I was having a good time already, a passenger enjoying the night.

Karen lit a cigarette from her soft-pack of Sportsman cigarettes, a portrait of a bridled horse's head in profile on the orange-and-white pack. She blew smoke at the ceiling and said, 'Do you enjoy your Tusker?'

'I do,' I said. 'It's good.'

'It's good Kenyan beer,' she said.

'You don't like beer?' I said to Flora.

'I do. But I'm drinking a wine cooler because I was beginning to get a bit of a Tusker-belly,' she said, patting her slim stomach.

The group at the other table had a small stereo and Jay-Z's *The Black Album* played.

'We'll drink here,' said Karen, 'then go to the studio, which isn't far. But there's a hip-hop group recording there now.'

'Are they good?' I said.

'They're okay,' said Flora, making a face at Karen.

'We don't like them that much,' said Karen. 'They're a little competitive.'

We finished our drinks and Karen hailed a car out front and we drove no more than five or six minutes and pulled up to a gate. Karen opened the padlocked gate with a small key, then we pulled into a large, empty dirt lot, the apartment building set back. I paid the driver. We walked to the building and from the lot it looked a little spooky, like it had been abandoned, paint peeling, scarred. We took the outdoor stairs up to an apartment and I didn't see a soul till Karen opened a door onto a smoky living room, where six or seven guys sat in the dark save the glow of a TV set. Hip hop played on blown speakers.

Karen and Flora said hello and introduced me and we were all greeted coldly, especially me. One guy in the corner, in a toque, with dreadlocks and bad teeth, was openly hostile toward me, sneering at me when Karen said, 'This is John.'

Somehow, I wanted to convey to this group of young men that I wasn't a tourist trying to sleep with their women — MC Karen and DJ Flora were very good-looking, but I was here as a friend, enjoying their company. But then again I didn't really care.

We went to another room that had been somewhat sound-proofed with foam and egg cartons stapled to the walls and there was an old mattress up against a wall, too, and a micro-phone in a stand.

'This is where we record vocals and instruments,' said Karen, and she opened a door to the adjacent room and said, 'And this is where we record and mix,' and there was a small mixing board and cables running into the room through a circular hole in the wall, which had been stuffed with socks and T-shirts.

'I'll be back,' said Karen and Flora and I were left standing in the room.

'Cool studio,' I said to Flora.

'It works,' she said. 'But it's annoying always sharing it.'

Karen returned and said. 'They're recording till at least midnight, so tonight doesn't look good. Let's smoke some ganja.'

We went out on the balcony, in the front of the apart-ment, and Karen produced a joint from her purse the size of a tampon. At first I refused the joint, thinking of Kenya's strict drug laws, which I'd been warned about, and thinking about Boris — that is, how embarrassed I'd be if I got in trouble with respect to drugs. Besides, I'd observed that people of a certain generation who lived in the former Soviet Union, although nonjudgmental when it came to over-indulging in spirits, were, say, e.g., extremely judgmental when it came to marijuana. But when I passed on the grass, Flora and Karen looked at me disapprovingly, like I was uncool, so I smoked some.

Staring out onto the empty parking lot, the night sky, we talked and smoked.

'When are you here till?' asked Flora.

'I leave on New Year's Eve.'

'Oh that's soon,' said Karen.

'Yes,' I said. 'It's a short trip, all things considered.'

'That's too bad,' she said.

'I might be back next year this time, too. I'll come back for the festival. And I'll stay longer next time.'

'That's in a year,' said MC Karen.

'Yes, that's not long,' I said.

They both laughed.

Flora said, 'In Nairobi, a year's a long time.'

'Why's that?'

'A lot happens in a year,' said Flora.

'Let's go to a club,' said MC Karen, and she called a car.

Erykah Badu's *Mama's Gun* played, 'Penitentiary Philosophy,' when we entered the packed, hot barroom. Karen cut a path through the crowd and got us a couple of seats at the bar. Flora saw a friend and went to talk to her. We sat on barstools and I shouted over the loud music, 'Good job!'

When the chorus hit, MC Karen stood on the rung of her stool and sang along. I desperately wanted to kiss her and she could tell and laughed and sat back down and slapped me on the back. She lit a Sportsman.

We drank beer and talked about art mainly; MC Karen's aspirations as an artist, specifically, bringing Kenyan music to the world, inspiring and healing the lonely, the hurt and the sick. She told me about *Sheng*, namely, the mixing of Kiswahili and English, in the hip-hop movement in Nairobi. Motivating people out of apathy, she said. Making people rejoice in their *Creator's glory*, she said. Empathy, she said, creating a sense of empathy for her fellow man, that was the task of the artist. I asked MC Karen her last name.

'Nyangweso,' she said.

'That's a beautiful name,' I said.

'I'm Luo, like Barack Obama,' she said, raising a fist. 'Like Raila Odinga.'

MC Karen told me that as an artist she's a warrior.

'I'm not much of a warrior,' I said, shyly, and smiled.

'You're an artist, John, like me,' she said. 'That means you're a warrior.'

MC Karen ordered us a couple of samosas from the bar and we rubbed salt on them and picked at them with our beers.

'You seem comfortable in Nairobi,' she said. 'You don't find it different?'

'Other than the portrait of Kibaki behind the bar,' I said, pointing upward at said portrait, 'this place isn't much different from bars back home.'

Eventually, I had to use the restroom and wound up having to urinate in a trough with several other young men. I looked at my watch and decided I should get back to the hotel soon.

When I returned to the bar MC Karen was standing with Flora.

'We ordered tequila shots,' said Flora.

'Okay,' I said, 'but then I should head back. It's late.'

We did the shots of tequila, with salt and lemon wedges, and I paid for them and for Flora's drinks, too, and MC Karen and I left without her. Flora stayed behind with her friends.

In the street outside the club, a small boy with burn marks on his face approached me asking for money, and I had my hand in a pocket to fish out money, when MC Karen rapidly chased him away, yelling something in Kiswahili. Her viciousness toward the boy startled me after her sermon on the importance of the artist's empathy and love and so on. She hailed a car and opened the door for me. I climbed in the backseat.

The car sat idling outside the gate as MC Karen went into an apartment building for god knows what reasons. She said she needed to stop somewhere and gave the driver directions. Other than the building, there was nothing around but brush. I listened to the cicadas' amazingly loud noisemakers. Or what I hoped were cicadas. Across the dark street, from behind the foliage, headlights flashed us. We heard a car door open and shut and a large man in linens leaned down to the driver's-side window. He spoke to the driver in Kiswahili and the driver answered some questions. They spoke for what seemed a long time, so I disassociated the best I could, thinking of my night with MC Karen. The man shone a flashlight in my face. I'd been warned about men posing as policemen but the driver said that the man was in fact a policeman, a plain-clothesman, and he let us wait for MC Karen.

After a few more minutes I messaged her: *Where r u.*

I thought she'd ditched me – at the side of the road, waiting outside a random apartment building, on the outskirts of Nairobi. But then she returned, smiling, as ever. And all was forgiven.

She got in the car and said, 'I know a place where we can eat – they're open all night – and we can get roast chicken and samosas and – '

'I'd love to keep going all night,' I said, 'but I'm flying out to Lamu tomorrow.'

'Okay,' she said. 'We'll get you back to the hotel.'

We rode back to the hotel in silence. MC Karen put her head in my lap and closed her eyes. My hand was on her shoulder, and I wanted the ride to last for hours.

When we pulled up to the hotel's gate I was disheartened. The security guard recognized me and opened the gate.

I said, 'Well, thank you.'

'Thank you,' she said. 'It was fun.'

Then she kissed me on the lips, a brief kiss.

'Goodnight,' I said, hesitated, then started to get out of the car.

'Do you have money for the driver?' she said.

I gave her two thousand Kenyan shillings and she said, 'More like three thousand.'

So I gave her another thousand and got out of the car.

'I'll SMS you while you're in Lamu,' she said. 'Goodnight, John!'

Back in my room I packed a knapsack full of clothing for Lamu. I lay on top of my sheets and looked at my Nokia. MC Karen had messaged me: *Thx for night :) c u soon.*

I faded off.

The flight out took longer than expected. There was a problem with the plane so we departed late, and then we were in the air for about two and a half hours. We flew out of a small airport, Wilson Airport, close to the hotel. But it'd been a long day, with a lot of waiting, which started with a quick trip into the city with Mark and Jason to a Nakumatt super-market. I bumped into the two at breakfast so we ate quickly and then took a car downtown. In front of the supermarket, which was inside a mall, sat a squat, robotic Santa Claus. *Ho ho ho*, it said, stiltedly, robotically, *ho ho ho*. And sleigh bell sound effects rattled and jangled and their relentless insistence sounded sinister, hair-raising, bone-chilling even, especially with the psychotic little Santa's *ho ho ho*. Santa looked dangerous, like sparks should come shooting out of its mouth, like it might burn the place down.

Everyone who passed the demon Santa Claus made comments, or terrified faces, laughing afterwards, so I knew I wasn't alone; I wasn't just imaging the festive fiend in front of the Nakumatt.

We walked down all the aisles but wound up only buying liquor. Mark and I, however, decided we'd come back to buy some coffee and tea as gifts. I wasn't sure what to buy, in terms of alcohol. I wasn't particularly excited to drink, so my heart wasn't in it.

'Try Kenya Cane,' said Jason. 'Have you tried Kenya Cane?'

'No.'

'It's kind of like a drug, more than alcohol.'

So I bought a bottle. And they bought a few bottles, a few different liquors.

'We're going to be in Lamu for Christmas,' said Jason. 'That's so awesome.'

Back at the hotel we waited for at least forty minutes in the lobby for the shuttle to the airport, approximately fifteen minutes away, and for people to get organized. I stood with Boris, dressed in his beachwear, that is, long linen shorts and a lightweight pale blue dashiki – he was excited to get to Lamu. He was happy and not overly perturbed with respect to the delays.

While we were waiting in the lobby, Boris poked my arm. 'You know who that is, right?' he said, discreetly motioning in the direction of a man walking away, his back in a blue blazer.

'Who?' I said.

'Ngũgĩ wa Thiong'o.'

I followed the back of this great writer as he made his way through the crowded lobby – the author of *Petals of Blood*, once imprisoned by Daniel arap Moi, Ngũgĩ had written a novel in Gikuyu on prison toilet paper and was later forced to live in exile, his books banned in Kenya for years. I got gooseflesh. Over the years I'd met some quote-unquote famous writers and artists but even catching a glimpse of Ngũgĩ affected me. Nothing like that had ever happened before. I felt a deep, instantaneous reverence for the man, even from only seeing his back.

But the rest of the day consisted of waiting, namely, waiting in the lobby, in the small airport terminal, on the sunny hot tarmac of the small runway, aboard the small plane on the runway; the flight, however, was spectacular, as we weren't that high up, so I watched the Kenyan landscape go by, more and more beautiful the closer we got to the coast.

We stood in an airfield, or an outdoor airport, as carts were loaded with our luggage, waiting to be ferried to the island. I had my luggage on me, one piece: my knapsack. I'd left my suitcase in storage at the hotel because we'd be back there in a few days before heading home. But my knapsack was overpacked, bursting at the seams. A writer from the U.S. south said, 'We don't need to worry about a bomb going off. It went off in your backpack.'

By the time we took the ferry – which was essentially a barge – from the airport – which was an open field – to the island, it was after nightfall. The ferrymen were referred to by those in the know as beach boys, that is to say, young athletic guys who spend their days playing Frisbee, smoking weed and performing tasks around the jetty, of myriad varieties.

The twelfth-century town of Lamu from the water on a dark night looked wondrous and beautiful, with its white buildings sparsely lit. The boat rocked as it slowed and approached a set of landing stairs, where it docked. Beach boys unloaded the luggage after we all disembarked, but I had my knapsack with me.

I stood beside Boris on the jetty, looking out at the *dhow*-speckled harbour, under a crescent moon and starry sky, and he said, 'Not bad, right?'

The boats rocked gently, some lit up, some shadowy, the sounds of the town behind us.

A boy, armed with a flashlight, guided me to my hotel. The group had significantly shrunk, but there were still far too many people to all stay in one of Lamu's many tiny hotels, so we were spread out around the island. I was staying in a place called Yumbe House, according to Anita Khalsa, who booked the rooms. The boy lit up the labyrinthine alleyways to Yumbe House, as we dodged donkeys and walked fast because it had started to rain. There were no cars on the island, though there were plenty of donkeys, and, *ergo*, plenty of donkey shit, which we sidestepped in the rainfall.

I kept thinking, *There's no way I'll ever remember the route to the hotel.*

The boy got me to the old stone hotel, where I attempted to tip him, and he refused my money, running away when I pulled out my wallet, and I checked in at the Staff House, a small hut made of bamboo and thatched, where a young thin man gave me a key with a wooden keychain. Checking in took all of a minute. I didn't give him any money, or my passport, simply said my name, and he walked me up a set of wooden stairs in the small courtyard, open to the elements, full of beautiful flora, to the second floor, where I was in room fourteen. The key on the wooden keychain opened the padlocked wooden door onto a small room, with a bed in white canopy mosquito netting, a little old worn desk for writing, or an escritoire, and there was an en suite washroom with a toilet, shower stall and sink. The walls didn't quite reach the thatched ceiling, so there was a gap, exposing the room to the outdoors, but that seemed necessary for air circulation. The floors were concrete, with a small throw rug near the bed.

'Perfect,' I said. '*Asante sana.*'

I was left alone in my room, which I'd immediately felt a connection to and affection for, and I sat down at the escritoire; the little scarred writing desk had a tiny lamp on top and several small drawers and it was near an outlet, though the power, I was warned, would go out every day for several hours – the island had brownouts, but the power always returned, for a few hours at least, so charge your laptop when you have the chance, I was told. I took my computer out of my bag and plugged it in. I worked on my piece about the festival for about an hour, and transcribed some notes from my notebook, when there was a knock on my door. It was Jason.

'Hey,' he said. 'Mark and I are staying here, too. We're just having drinks across the way,' he said, pointing to the other side of the courtyard, 'where there's sort of a common area up top, with chairs and day-beds. It's covered. You should join us.'

I told him I'd be there in a minute and he said not to bother bringing booze, they'd already cracked a bottle of

Kenya Cane, so I saved my notes and put on some Muskol mosquito repellent, did a few quick push-ups, locked up, and made my way across the courtyard.

It was raining hard and there were a few leaks in the thatch, but we were happy to be in Lamu and immediately high on the Kenya Cane mixed with lime soda. Jason smoked Marlboro Lights and after a while, after several drinks, Mark smoked them, too. Boris called my cell and I told him what we were up to, but he said he'd stay in, get some much-needed sleep and wait out the rain. He was staying at Petley's Inn, he said, which faced the sea and had a bar. He had air-conditioning, he told me, but didn't like the feel of it. We agreed I'd stop by tomorrow.

'It's after midnight,' said Jason. 'Merry Christmas!'

The muezzin's call to prayer from a loudspeaker atop a minaret woke me early in the morning, though its echoing, hypnotic music put me right back to sleep. I woke again to the call to prayer, but it was many hours later. I was covered in sweat but it was hot. I sat up, under the mosquito netting, and realized we were in Lamu.

And it was Christmas.

I picked up my Nokia from the bedside table and saw there were six missed calls from Boris and two text messages: *Where r u* and *R u ok*, respectively.

So I called him back.

'Hey,' I said, when he picked up.

'Hey man, so you're okay?'

'Fine. Yeah sorry. I guess I slept in.'

'It's two in the afternoon,' he said. 'You missed the greetings.'

'Yes, sorry, I know. I just haven't been sleeping,' I said.

'It's okay, man. We're heading down the coast to a small

village at three-thirty, where we'll eat and stuff. It's like an hour or so by boats. Should be all right.'

'Okay,' I said.

'So we're leaving from the jetty at three-thirty,' said Boris. 'I'll be there.'

When I hung up I put on some shorts and went in search of water and something small to eat. I walked out of the courtyard and into the narrow streets of Lamu. I turned a few corners and there were commercial stalls everywhere, selling colourful cloths of various varieties, wooden curios, from sculptures to dinnerware, and silver, a lot of silverwork. But amongst the stalls and the ceaseless calls of the bazaar, I spotted a shop that sold corner-store items – chocolate bars and aspirin and cigarettes, et cetera. I bought two large bottles of water for the room and a Snickers bar. Across from him a stall sold samosas, so I bought two and started to make my way back to Yumbe House. After turning down a few streets and realizing I was walking in circles, as the same retailers vied for my attention, a small boy asked me what I was looking for. I said, *Yumbe House*. And he walked me back to the old stone edifice.

In my room, I ate my samosas and Snickers and took my pills and freshened up for the trip down the coast. Then, sitting on my bed, I fell asleep.

I woke up to hard knocking on my door. I sat up startled. It was Mark and Jason.

'I missed the boat, didn't I?' I said.

'Yes,' they said.

'But we're taking a smaller, faster boat,' said Jason.

'And we're leaving now,' said Mark.

'Great!' I said. 'I'm ready to go.'

Down at the jetty, we boarded a small boat with an outboard engine and we put on lifejackets and a slim older man piloted the boat.

We were travelling fast along the coastline, the wind blasting our faces fresh, the sun starting to set. I sat on the bow seat, alone, Jason and Mark behind me, the ship's pilot at the stern, his hand on the tiller. The only sounds were those of the engine and wind and they were like excited meditative silence. My heart raced.

I stepped out of the boat and into the ocean. There wasn't a dock, so the boat couldn't take us right up to the beach, so we got out about a hundred metres from land and started walking shoreward in the ocean.

From the beach, we walked for about fifteen minutes into the brush until we reached a clearing, with a fire blazing, a band playing, dancing, and kids kicking around a football.

'We made it,' said Mark. 'How's this for a Christmas dinner!'

There were coolers of beer and bottled water. We each grabbed a beer.

Boris spotted me and I approached him and said, 'Sorry about that, man. I don't know what came over me. Like, hardcore fatigue.'

'How're you feeling now?' he said.

'Good, man, good.'

'Well, good,' he said.

'Anyway, Merry Christmas!' I said.

'Ha yes. Two Jews celebrating, one a Soviet Jew, the other Canadian, celebrating Christmas in an East African village on the Indian Ocean. Somewhat random,' he said.

'Yes,' I said. 'It is.'

The sky darkened and sparks flew skyward.

I felt a football hit the back of my legs, so I turned around and pinned the ball under my foot. Stanley stood with a young boy, both waiting for me to kick the ball back into play, so I passed it to Stanley, who overtook the boy and scored on his net, which was delineated by two rocks with a space of approximately two metres between them.

Stanley, the boy and I kicked the ball around for a half-hour or so. The kid was a good footballer but very cheeky, in general, at one point posing for a photo with Stanley and me, making rabbit ears behind my head, his arm stretched high. I had my revenge, though, when I scored on his net several times in a row. He wasn't much of a goalkeeper. He winded me, however, and I had to quit. I'd worked up too much of a sweat and regretted it.

Four men, two for each fish, carried massive red snappers to the fire and set them up on spits. A table was set up with rice and *ugali* and collard greens. People lined up with paper plates. The fishes turned in the fire.

I ate only a little of the fish, a few forkfuls, though it was delicious, thinking about how Saul Bellow almost died as the result of toxoplasmosis, from eating red snapper. The parasitic disease was rare and I didn't think I'd get it from the fish but I didn't want to eat much, even though it tasted good.

Drinking more beer, I looked at my Nokia and I'd received a message from MC Karen: *Merry Xmas! xx*

So I wrote: *Merry Xmas to you too! Lamu's beautiful.*

And then I called my girlfriend, Stacey, back in Montreal.

She picked up and I wished her Merry Christmas. It was loud where she was, at her aunt's house – she seemed harried and distant – and so we didn't talk long, only for a few minutes. I walked off, away from the fire, away from the crowd, and excitedly told her where I was, that is to say, I told her I didn't even really know where I was, and I looked up at the night sky and tried to describe it to her. I felt myself becoming emotional, missing her terribly, trying to tell her that, but then she said she had to go; more family had arrived.

I said I understood and I said *I love you* and she said *I love you* and that was that. I went back to the fire, stopping at a large cooler, pulling out a fresh wet Tusker.

Boris and Stanley and I stood and watched people dance around the fire as we drank our beers.

'Look at these *wazungu*,' said Stanley, shaking his head, as we watched middle-aged writers dance around the fire as the band sang with drums.

'I'm not circling the fire dancing,' I said.

'You're not a *mzungu*,' he said.

'Thank you!' I said.

Kenneth walked toward us from the fire and said, 'Guys, I want you to meet a good friend of mine.' A tall slightly hunched man, in a T-shirt and a *kikoy*, turned around from facing the fire and looked our way, and Kenneth said, 'This is my good friend Osama.' The man walked toward us and at first appeared as a tall broad silhouette. 'This is Osama Goldberg,' said Kenneth.

'*As-salamu-alaykum*,' he said. 'Hi.'

'*Wa-alaykum-salaam*,' we said.

We sat on log benches, low to the ground, around the fire pit, listening to Osama Goldberg's story, namely, how a middle-class Jewish guy from the U.S. wound up living in Lamu as a Muslim. Osama was born Nathan Jonathan Goldberg in 1956, in New York City where he lived in Brooklyn till he was twelve, then moving with his mom and her new husband to Hollywood, Florida, in 1968, where his stepfather was a developer in Broward County and adjacent Miami-Dade County, too. He briefly attended the University of

Miami, starting a BA, but dropped out after two years, staying, however, a Hurricanes fan, he said, referencing his T-shirt. He told us he'd tried everything and travelled everywhere – doing peyote in New Mexico with mystics, hanging out in California ashrams, travelling to Japan in the late eighties, walking vast stretches of the Great Wall of China, visiting Jerusalem and the Wailing Wall – but it wasn't till he'd arrived in Lamu, backpacking, in 1991, that he felt like he'd found his home on Earth. The ways of the island, he said, so laid-back but spiritual, were attractive to him. 'It's a simple lifestyle on Lamu,' he said. '*Pole pole*'s the mantra, for everyone, which means *slowly*, like take it easy, in Kiswahili.' Osama learned Kiswahili and Arabic and became deeply engaged in Quranic studies, attending a *madrassa* at the Riyadha Mosque, 'an engagement that only continues to deepen,' he said. 'I know the Quran by heart. I'm *hafiz*. But millions know it by heart.'

Osama, too, had become an expert in Lamu's history and was the island's most visible celebrity, known to all the islanders as the Mayor of Lamu.

'Lamu,' he said, 'has been coastal East Africa's major port of shipment and trade since the 1300s. It's the oldest Swahili settlement in Kenya.' He leaned in, closer to the firelight. 'The Arab world, however, always moved through Lamu, hence the over twenty mosques on the small island today,' he said. 'Later, the Portuguese invaded in the sixteenth century, then the Turkish helped take Lamu back in the seventeenth century,' he said, sipping on bottled water. 'The island's seen everything, and everybody, from the Turks to the Germans to the Chinese, over the centuries. But it's been a capital of poetry, education, art and religion the whole time. Lamu's always been simultaneously traditional and cutting-edge, a bit avant-garde.' Osama looked up at us and, somewhat dismayed, said, 'Nonetheless, the slave trade flourished in

Lamu for centuries. Everything's been traded through Lamu, including people. The ivory trade, too, flourished here.' No one spoke while the Mayor of Lamu had the floor. 'The world has passed through Lamu but nothing can alter the island.' He smiled. 'It's the greatest, most accepting place on earth.'

We were interrupted by Anita Khalsa's announcement that the boats were heading back to the main island in a half-hour, so we should start to make our way to the beach.

'Also,' Anita said loudly, 'to alleviate some of your worries regarding terrorism. Some of you have approached me concerned because you heard the Taliban are in and around Lamu, along the coast and so on. Well, not to worry; it's not the Taliban you read about in the papers and hear about on TV. They're simply local youths who thought *Taliban* made a cool gang name.'

People were gathering their gear, starting to clean up the area, and I asked Boris, 'Do you think there are terrorists in the region? Supposedly Lamu's a hideout, which makes sense. Hard place to find someone.'

'I think weapons move through Lamu but they're never used here. You heard Osama: everything moves through here. It's an extremely peaceful place, though. It literally has zero crime. I saw Chris Matthews vacationing here years ago, the *Hardball* guy, you know? He used to be a Peace Corps guy,' said Boris.

'Was he talking unnaturally loudly?' I said.

'Ha. No. You could tell he wanted to travel incognito.'

'What do you make of Osama?' I said.

'Seems like an interesting guy,' said Boris. 'Some Jews have an amazing ability to take on other cultures.'

'He's gone deep,' I said, 'learning Kiswahili and Arabic and converting to Islam.'

'Yeah, interesting,' said Boris.

'He took peyote in New Mexico in '78 and woke up in Lamu in '91.'

'Not a bad life, I'm sure,' said Boris. 'Beats Hollywood, Florida.'

Stanley caught up with us as we walked back to the beach, following a flashlight's path, with a bottle of Kenya Cane in his hand.

'Would you like a drink?' he said, offering me the bottle. 'Brother Osama probably wouldn't approve, but between us it's cool.'

I took the bottle and took a deep swig, then offered it to Boris.

'No thank you,' he said, waving it off. So I passed it back to Stanley, who took another sip.

We were travelling back on a large sailboat, one presumably equipped with an engine, but we had to take a small rowboat to the sailboat, due to the shallowness of the water; the rowboat made several trips to the sailboat. In order to get to the rowboat, however, we needed to wade into the ocean.

'I can't swim,' said Stanley, and he clutched my hand tightly as we waded deeper and deeper into the water. It was dark and I couldn't remember the last time I'd held a grown man's hand, not since I was a boy, though I was glad I could provide Stanley with some sense of security and it cheered me up a little. The dark sky and the dark ocean were one, horizonless, as we walked into the void holding hands.

By the time we reached the small boat, we were more than waist-deep in the ocean. Jason helped pull us into the rowboat. We were rowed over to the sailboat, the oarlocks squeaking loudly, and we climbed a rope-ladder to board the ship.

Eventually, when everyone was aboard, we set sail for Lamu.

I sat up top, lying on the deck with Mark and Jason and Stanley, staring up at the sky, as we passed the Kenya Cane back and forth, dipping with the vessel's prow, occasionally, as we glided fast along the sea. I sat up and looked over the edge and thought about slipping off. If there were a gangplank, I'd walk it, I thought. This felt like a clean place to disappear, no one having to deal with my remains, so far away from family that it would all almost seem like a dream, and the sharks would make short order of my body, as it sank into the dark ocean.

Back in my room at Yumbe House, I waved my hand in front of my face and there were wild trails, my fingers leaving impressions in their wake, like the handful of times I had done acid as a teenager. If one good thing came out of my adolescent drug experimentation, however, it was the knowledge that if anything weird occurs with respect to your mind and/or vision and you're on any type of drugs and/or alcohol, it's just the drugs and/or alcohol and there's no reason to freak out: freaking out, in fact, makes everything much worse. And if you're in a safe place, enjoy the trip. So I got into bed, under the netting, and listened to some music.

I put on Joanna Newsom's new album, Ys, to try and fall asleep to, but I ended up listening to many of the songs several times and finding myself occasionally a little lachry-mose again, or at least choked up. I sat in the dark, my back propped up against the headboard, under the mosquito netting, listening to the music. When the album finished, I played it again, without moving, though sipping from the bottle of water on my bedside table. I listened carefully, though my mind would wander, thinking of my life back home, a life I didn't know what to make of.

In my dreams, Osama Goldberg had me by the throat, and his head cocked back as he choked me and I saw into his nostrils, which had silver coins lodged deep inside them, shining, nevertheless, catching the sunrays, reflecting them back at me blindingly, and Osama said, '*Hapo sawa!*' He squeezed tighter. '*Usilie!*'

I awoke gasping for air, gnashing my teeth, immediately thinking that I'd never had a dream with such tactility – I felt Osama's hands around my neck like one feels a tabletop. I was soaking wet. My left arm was strangely stiff and my left thumb had seized up completely; I'd probably slept on it, I thought, but I started worrying something horrible was happening to my arm. The bruising had barely faded.

After chugging water, I forced myself to lie back down for a few hours, tossing around, though staying in bed.

In the morning, I got up and went down to the courtyard, and it turned out that a simple breakfast of tea and toast and mango was included with the room so I ate, took my pills, and then walked over to the seafront to Boris's hotel.

Petley's Inn was more upscale than Yumbe House, but I liked the simplicity of Yumbe House better. At Petley's there was a pool, though, and a bar that looked onto the ocean. Boris and I reclined on high couches, a tea table between us, in Petley's second-floor bar, drinking tea and bottled water, the sea air blowing through the barroom, which had no glass windows – instead it was open air, the sounds of the water-front beneath us.

'Later this afternoon, Kenneth's friend Osama has offered to take some of us on a boat tour of the region. He's got a *dhow* or something,' said Boris. 'You're welcome to come.'

'I might sit the trip out,' I said. 'I'm worried about seasickness.'

I'm not sure why I said that but I did.

'Makes sense,' said Boris.

Between the hangover from the Christmas celebrations and whatever I was experiencing, I felt terrible, as I sat drinking tea with Boris, looking out onto the sea, the sun shining, the perfect day, the shining sea giving off a blinding, twinkling glare. Sunrays got caught up in the haze from the heat, a superabundance of sun. I was acutely aware of the vast discrepancy between how I felt on the inside and how glorious it was outside, isolated by my condition, which I didn't feel comfortable sharing with anybody; Boris, on the other hand, seemed so joyful, vibrant, flourishing, incandescent. In other words, all the things he wasn't back in Montreal's wintry climate; back home he seemed, well, so Russian. Here, on this remote island on the Indian Ocean, he seemed the picture of good health and levity, the brooding, often morbid, mind now slanted toward a more don't-worry-be-happy ease and contentment, without any cheesiness. His blissful sense of being, however, only partially quelled my distemper. My paranoia was off the charts and I couldn't tell anyone about it. I was too embarrassed and positive it was the antimalarials; but they were in my bloodstream, I'd been taking them for days, so there was nothing I could do. Knowing that one's psychic unravelling is the result of a drug, sadly, doesn't stop one from psychically unravelling. I'd have to avoid people and skip events.

We lay back, Boris relaxed and elevated by the sublimity of our surroundings, me tensed up, feeling vertiginous fear like I was going to fall off the high couch.

I walked Boris down to the jetty and we stood staring at the donkeys. The donkeys were everywhere.

'Supposedly there are over three thousand donkeys on the island,' Boris said.

'That's amazing,' I said. 'I saw one carrying cinderblocks on the way here.'

Boris said, 'Hey man, is it just me or is there something distinctly Jewish looking about these donkeys?'

We both laughed and I left him at the jetty waiting for Osama and company, and I started making my way back to Yumbe House.

I decided I'd lie low till the barbecue and party later in the evening, on Manda Island, at Diamond Beach Village.

Leaving the jetty, I walked inland, back to the mazes, trying to negotiate the city's core. There were many beautiful things for sale – some of the nicest, more ornately wood-carved furniture I'd ever seen, for example, and plenty of jewellery, beaded and silver – but I wasn't in the mood to buy.

Then, I spotted Stanley walking by the various sellers and he smiled at me.

'John, man, how're you?' he said. 'You've survived Lamu so far.'

'Barely,' I said. 'But I'm all right.'

'I'm just on my way to Jannat House, the inn I'm staying at, to drop off some papers,' he said, referencing a full folder under his arm. 'But then I'm going to watch some football. Do you want to join me?'

'I'll walk you to Jannat House,' I said. 'What's the football match?'

'Well, I'm a Chelsea fan,' he said, 'because of Boris, actually, and my predilection for all things Russian. Roman Abramovich, Chelsea's owner, kind of looks like our comrade Boris and he's a Russian Jew, too.'

'I think that's where the commonalities end,' I said.

'Maybe, ha,' said Stanley, 'but there's a place that's playing videos of the game from a few days ago, Wigan Athletic and Chelsea, and another match, too. Anyway, I missed the match and don't know the outcome, so I bought a ticket earlier to watch it in a little theatre this afternoon.'

'That's really cool,' I said, as we walked to Jannat House. 'How're your accommodations?'

'Nice,' said Stanley, 'but I get tired of Lamu very quickly.'

'Really, why? It's beautiful.'

'It is. But I get sick of the donkey shit. I'm a city guy,' he said.

Like many of the buildings in Lamu, Jannat House was very white, with thatched roofs, and it had a courtyard with a little pool and a window where one could order drinks: Stanley ordered a beer and I ordered a bottle of water, not wanting to drink early in the afternoon.

We sat by the pool and chatted for a while. I told Stanley I hadn't been feeling well and that I thought maybe the malaria medication had something to do with it.

'Are you taking anything?' I asked.

'No,' he said. 'It never even crossed my mind.'

He went to get ready for his football match and I headed back to Yumbe House. I told him I'd see him down at the jetty, around seven, when we were taking a boat to Manda Island.

Back in the streets I heard a seller yell, 'You, the Canadian, come here,' he said. So I stopped and turned around.

'How'd you know I was Canadian?' I said.

'Lucky guess,' said the man standing behind his counter, with shiny silverwork everywhere on black fabric. 'My name's Slim.'

'John,' I said.

'Nice to meet you, John,' he said. 'Are you looking for anything? A gift for a girlfriend?'

'I don't think so.'

'Oh come on. I'm sure you are. How about a nice ring,' he said. 'I'll sell it cheap. Very cheap. It's beautiful work. I'm an expert silversmith. And it's very inexpensive here. This ring,' he said, holding up a small weaved silver ring, 'only thirty American dollars.'

'I'll give you twenty,' I said.

'For forty I'll give you this ring and these earrings,' he said, holding a simple but elegant pair of dangling silver earrings.

'Thirty,' I said.

'No, John, forty's a good deal. The ring's thirty dollars, which is a good price, and the earrings are thirty-five dollars, which is also a good price, and it'd be much more expensive in the United States. Or Canada, sorry,' he said.

'All right,' I said, 'forty dollars.'

'Nice doing business with you, John,' he said, and started carefully wrapping the jewellery, and putting it in plastic Ziploc baggies. 'Send me a postcard,' he said, handing me a business card. 'I have postcards from everywhere.' He motioned to postcards pinned up to the borders of his booth. 'What city do you live in in Canada?'

'Montreal.'

'I've already got postcards from Montreal and Toronto,' he said. 'Can you send me one from Calgary? I don't have one from Calgary.'

I'd no intention of buying anything but Slim quickly had convinced me and, besides, his jewellery was appealing, though I remembered Stacey didn't like jewellery, but it didn't matter, I thought, someone would want it.

Somehow, while daydreaming, I made it back to Yumbe House unassisted. And I felt a genuine sense of satisfaction. I thought I'd try and nap before the party.

We arrived at Diamond Beach at dusk. Bamboo torches lit the way from the beach in the semidarkness to the village. Again, we'd taken a large sailboat, then a small rowboat to the shore, though Manda Island was very close and we could see Lamu from the beach, and I kept thinking about all the people over the centuries viewing the island *entrepôt* for the first time from the sea.

It was the starriest night yet. We were all excited. A bonfire blazed as we walked up to the resort village. There were barbecues cooking up meats and fishes and we were served drinks immediately, a sort of punch.

There were Christmas lights, too, around some of the buildings, powered by a generator.

A young woman in a *kikoy* and a bikini top welcomed us as we piled into the village, and she told us about how she visited Lamu backpacking, in the late nineties, for Y2K, in fact, and she'd decided to make Lamu her home. She'd been back to the U.K. twice in the seven years since she'd moved, but Manda Island's now her home, she told us, and that's why she'd opened the resort, a resort built like a Swahili village. Indeed, it was beautiful and simple there. 'Today, also,' she said, 'is the first day of Kwanzaa. So happy Kwanzaa to all of you here, especially our American guests.'

A mix of mostly reggae and pop played as people ate and mingled and danced. I approached Boris, who introduced me to a young South African poet named Max in a HIV POSITIVE T-shirt. Max had flown in from Johannesburg for the festival and we made small talk for a few minutes and then Max moved on. Boris looked a little sunburnt, and I asked him how his boat trip went.

'Oh amazing, man. Osama really is an expert in the region. Nice smart guy, really,' said Boris. 'And he may not drink but he had one of those, like, fishing boxes ... '

'A tackle box.'

'Yeah he had a tackle box full of different marijuanas and hashishes and smoked all day long,' said Boris. 'He's a hippie.'

'I think he hates me like poison,' I said.

'What are you talking about?'

'Are you taking antimalarials?' I asked.

'No,' he said. 'I never do. They have them around if you get malaria and need them.'

Then, a poet, Ed, from the southern United States, joined us.

'Hey, Ed,' said Boris. 'We're just talking about malaria.'

'I got malaria in Uganda,' said Ed, 'years ago.'

'Are you serious?' Boris said.

'Yes, it was serious. I wasn't anywhere near a hospital so the villagers took care of me. I was delirious and people kept bringing me these sugar cakes. I was so feverish, sweating nonstop, having wild nightmares, which seemed so real, terrifying, and one night I thought I was in the hut but I woke up in the middle of a dirt road a mile or so from the village.'

'What happened?' said Boris.

'I walked back to the village and eventually my fever went down and I could travel to a hospital and start my antimalarials. In the end I was fine, though I lost, like, twenty pounds, which I didn't have to lose.'

'Are you taking anything now?' I said.

'No,' said Ed. 'I mean, the cure for malaria's a double-dose of the antimalarials for a cycle.'

I excused myself and walked down to the beach. I sat on a woodpile and attempted to equilibrate. I stared upward at the starred black infinity, the most tremendous view of the heavens I'd ever seen, but I couldn't shake fear.

Due to my course of medications and vaccinations, I thought, I'd developed an iatrogenic illness. *There's nothing to be afraid of*, I thought. 'There's nothing to be afraid of,' I said.

Standing, I decided to walk down the beach, with my head skyward. The sky was dark, black, studded with bright stars, and the sky's arch seemed more prevalent here than anywhere else in the world, concave like the Cinesphere I visited as a child at Toronto's Ontario Place, the planetarium's show projected on the curved screen. And I kept walking down the beach, thinking, gazing up at the stars, but then I heard rustling and a woman and a man, I thought, and I thought I saw the beast with two backs, so I turned around.

The starry water sparkled up the beach reflecting starlight.

I stood at the edge of the water, looking up, letting the tide lap up against my shoes, pulling me, gently, into the phosphorescent ocean. I stood transfixed by the lightshow, the sky and sea twinkling before me.

Laughter startled me out of my spacey reverie. A woman ran past me, in her bra and underwear, and into the flitting luminous water.

I turned around and there were others, dropping trou, running past me and into the water, laughing, screaming, splashing, joyous. Then I saw Boris, throwing off his dashiki, splashing into the phosphorescence in his shorts. He swam out. I heard his disembodied voice from the water say, 'John, come on in! It's wonderful!'

'Maybe in a minute,' I lamely said and I heard some calls of encouragement and some groans. I turned around and walked back up to the village.

At the bar, I ordered a bottle of water. I walked around the premises, breathing deeply, trying to let all the beauty pull me out of my own head. But it was difficult – I wasn't the master of my own house. Something had infected my brain.

Beach boys danced by the fire dressed up as female belly dancers, their faces veiled, their muscular midriffs exposed. People watched and smiled, their faces contorting in the torchlight and firelight. One beach boy, dressed up, started spinning fire, a poi performance, making wild fiery geometrical shapes in the air.

A crowd gathered.

Things seemed eerie and the light and shadows were doing strange things as the beach boy, in sheer fabrics, spun the fire. If Banquo's ghost had appeared I wouldn't have been surprised.

Elizabeth, the *Esquire* writer, jumped into the centre of the crowd and took the fire from a veiled beach boy dancing in a dress and started spinning the blazing fuel-soaked wicks like a poi pro. Fiery flowers glowed in the air.

Kenneth came up beside me and said, 'Are you having fun? You're looking a little dewy,' he added.

'Yes,' I said, 'but it's unfair to take advantage of a village full of tourists on antimalarials with hallucinogenic pyrotechnics.'

'You have a way with words, man,' he said.

But I was dead serious.

'Come sit with us and have a drink,' said Kenneth, leading me to a fireside picnic table.

I sat down with Kenneth and a friend of his, Ciku, and Osama Goldberg, who was telling stories and had Ciku in stitches. Kenneth introduced me.

'I remember you from last night,' said Osama. 'How's it going, man? Are you enjoying Lamu?'

'I am, thank you,' I said.

Boris walked up from the beach and joined us, his hair wet from the ocean, a sense of salty vitality about him.

'Do you ever miss drinking?' Ciku asked Osama as she sipped punch.

'No, I had my days of devilry,' said Osama. 'But those days are over.'

I looked under the picnic table at his feet but they weren't cloven, though his big toe was separated from the rest of the toes in his flip-flop sandals.

'I'm a father now,' said Osama. 'Religion's good for a family man.'

'How many children do you have?' said Ciku.

'Two daughters. One daughter who's fourteen, Maira, with one of my wives. And with my other wife I have another daughter, Aisha, who's ten. She just turned ten.'

Everyone nodded politely, though I think we were all surprised that he had two wives. And I was afraid I betrayed my surprise.

We got on to politics and the Bush administration.

'When I look at Bush and Cheney,' said Osama, 'I know I made the right decision moving to Lamu and converting to Islam. Those two are the worst terrorists on earth.'

No one said anything, though there was no love for Bush et al. at the table.

Osama said, 'U.S. involvement in Iraq has been a disaster. Also, their backing of Israel.'

And his eyes shifted toward me, narrowing, sharp blue.

'I've never been,' I said, my voice breaking. 'To Israel, that is.'

Osama's neck snapped back in the direction of Boris, Ciku and Kenneth and he once again seemed jovial.

I couldn't shake the feeling that Osama Goldberg had anti-Semitic feelings toward me, though not Boris, perhaps because he's a Russian Jew, I thought, a priori not subjected to a Jewish education but certainly persecution for being a Jew. Osama liked Boris, it was obvious. But it was equally obvious that he despised me, or so I thought. And my bones were chilled and I shook a little, though nobody seemed to notice. It was dark but we sat under the universe, by the fire, and the universe was on display, a starlit sky, forever, never stopping, so many stars that when I moved quickly, while looking up at the sky, there was no gap between the stars, the light was one, one blur but one.

When he looked at me I could tell Osama Goldberg didn't only see a non-Muslim man-boy but a lousy Jew, a disaffected diaspora Jew, who barely knows a word of Hebrew, basically memorizing his Torah and *haftarah* portions for his Bar Mitzvah day, forgetting everything, immediately thereafter, his brain as inconstant as an Etch A Sketch, that he'd studied with his rabbi, who put so much time and energy into the boy, only for him to end up an irreligious piece of shit. An effete Jew, a useless Jew, bookish without utility, now on the east coast of Africa briefly, only to leave no impact on this land of limitless and varied cultures, a land that wants no truck with this spectral embodiment of nothingness.

Osama's eyes said so much – slits, pinched tightly, though emitting so much sharp light, like the crescent moon above us.

Before travelling, I'd read David Mamet's latest book, *The Wicked Son: Anti-Semitism, Self-Hatred, and the Jews*, and I think it gave me a complex about not being Jewish enough – that is to say, Mamet's bullying of Jews not interested in regularly attending *shul* did its job, and I hated myself sufficiently for being lost, a Jew without Judaism. I needed to commit to something, I thought, a religion. I needed to be more like Osama Goldberg, I thought. *No one likes an unaligned assimilationist like me.*

'Excuse me,' I said, abruptly standing up.

Kenneth raised an eyebrow and stared.

'Sorry,' I said. 'I just have to go to the washroom.'

I went off in some brush and urinated and, for the billionth time, tried to pull myself together.

When Anita Khalsa made the announcement that we were heading back to Lamu, I felt a great sense of relief. I was one of the first on the rowboat to the sailboat. I sat on a bench on the boat, waiting for the others to climb aboard, biding my time. Boris and Stanley were the last to be transported to the sailboat. Stanley stood up in the small boat, extending his hand to be helped out onto the big boat, tipping the small boat with Boris still onboard. Stanley made it onto the big boat without getting a splash of water on him. Boris emerged from the ocean laughing, pulling himself back onto the rowboat.

When we disembarked, I didn't go to Petley's, where many were heading for a nightcap, and I didn't head back to Yumbe House right away; instead, I decided to sit alone on a concrete bench at the jetty, looking out onto the sea. I stared at the stars trying to collect myself. As I stared, the stars began to whirl. I closed my eyes, finding all the light dizzying, and when I opened my eyes I saw Osama.

Osama's silhouette stalked the seascape. His stride long, in a *kikoy*, his head turning to face me, staring me down, as he walked. It was dark but I could feel his eyes pinning me to the concrete bench. At one point, due to the intensity, I closed my eyes. It took my breath away, briefly, that is, my breath was taken away, from somewhere, and then it snapped back inside me, with a terrifying shock, an intimation of nothing, when it'd be taken for good. When I opened my eyes, Osama was farther along the jetty, walking, no longer staring me down.

I waited ten minutes, then made my way back to Yumbe House.

Back at the inn, Jason and Mark were having a drink on the day-beds, talking about their shared childhood and adolescence. They invited me to join them.

Jason said, 'Boris says you're not feeling great.'

I felt a little choked up; Jason seemed so nice.

'I think the antimalarials might be getting to me,' I said, quietly, embarrassed, afraid that if I spoke too much tears would follow.

Jason smiled, the friendly, comforting smile of a young Nathan Lane.

'Seriously,' he said, 'stop taking the antimalarials. If you get malaria, we'll get you medication, but in the meantime stop taking them. The side effects can be really terrible –

like, people have psychotic reactions. You're going to be fine, but stop taking them now.'

I was so grateful to Jason – and to his second cousin, Nathan Lane – because I believed him. I finally believed everything would be all right.

They sat up talking and drinking and I gave them my bottle of Kenya Cane and I drank water till I was sleepy, then I hit the hay, excited to be leaving Lamu the next day, ready to get back to Nairobi, then Amsterdam and Montreal.

I stopped taking my meds and didn't drink for the rest of the trip, either. When we were back in Nairobi, back at the Heron Court Hotel, I read *Half of a Yellow Sun* and didn't socialize much save dinner at Galina and Martin's house with Sveta and Alexi and Tanya and Boris.

Then it was time to leave Nairobi.

Again, we had a long layover in Amsterdam but not as long as on the way there, so there was no need for a day-room. We ate overpriced sandwiches, which Boris generously bought, and Tanya and I walked around the gift shops as Boris checked his email and surfed the internet.

Saddam Hussein had been hanged the day before and I didn't know about it. It was on the cover of every newspaper – *The New York Times*, *The Wall Street Journal*, *De Telegraaf*, *Haaretz*, *Le Monde*, *El País* – all with images of Saddam. They did it, I thought, and wasted no time. They executed him.

Holding Tanya's hand, a young woman walked past us, in her early twenties, I guessed, wearing a T-shirt that said *F★CK*, and I hoped Tanya didn't read her shirt. But then she said, 'You're never a star when you use that kind of language.'

'You're right,' I said. 'So true!'

We waited around for our plane. The Amsterdam sky was grey, for it had been raining lightly. I stood at the giant window looking out onto the runways. The light grey sky streaked with white and dark clouds looked like cold hard marble.

Our flight was called.

When we landed it was nighttime and snowing in Montreal. Our luggage arrived fairly quickly and we breezed through customs.

I spotted Nina waiting for us on the other side of the gate, and when Nina saw Tanya her eyes were full of tears and she was smiling, holding her hands up to her chin, patiently waiting and holding back her excitement to see her child. As soon as we were through passport control and on the other side of the gate, Tanya made a mad dash for her mother and Nina picked her up in her arms, squeezing her tightly, then putting Tanya down; Nina kneeled and cleared the hair away from her daughter's face, taking her face in, examining it, and she smiled tearfully, kissed her and then embraced her tightly, the two cheek to cheek, holding each other. I choked up and I could tell Boris choked up, too.

I said I'd grab a cab and Boris laughed and said, 'Don't be silly, man. We'll drive you home.'

I was back in my apartment by eight that evening, giving me enough time to shower before meeting my girlfriend at a party, a party to ring in the new year, though I wasn't in a partying mood. I knew things between Stacey and me were finished.

JENNY

'I find pretty much everybody I've ever cared about disappointing,' said Jenny, 'and it's always been this way, even when I was a little kid. No one can love you the way you want to be loved. It's just another sad fact.'

'There are two types of people: one, those who believe in an afterworld and the various sets of rules one has to live by to get to said afterworld, even if those rules hurt others; and, then, two: those who don't believe in an afterworld and within that group many would like to enact the dichotomy of heaven and hell here on earth because they won't get the satisfaction in the afterlife because they don't believe in one. Regardless, that makes for a hell of a lot of people who don't care about others and only care about getting their just deserts, whether here on earth or in the heaven that awaits. And I don't see much else going on.'

'No, I hate cocaine. It gives people a false sense of accomplishment. Which makes them super obnoxious. But go ahead if you want.'

'Just a couple of beers.'

'Sometimes I think I associate heartbreak with having zero appetite and getting skinny just so I put it in a positive light.

Who wants to be in love and content and getting plump on turkey,' she said.

'No, he died in '63. All right. Sure.'

'People aren't interested in the truth. They're interested in preserving their own narcissism – keeping it intact, whatever the cost ...'

'*Babe* and *The Mother and the Whore*.'

'Tastes like diesel fuel.'

'Jews have been historically seen as obstacles to ridiculous fantasies,' she said, 'but that doesn't mean they haven't manufactured their own equally ridiculous fantasies. Israel, for example.'

'People just want to get famous, like it'll save them, even if the reasons for getting famous are ignominious. It's actually a boring topic and for stupid people, like God.'

'I don't know. I kind of find sex boring,' she said. 'Like, cocks are fascinating, I guess, but also gross, and they make you pregnant and ruin your life and at best give you a home filled with children and a fat husband who all resent you. And ruin your body, of course. But, yeah, I kind of like to give blowjobs, though.'

'I actually find Jews really annoying, too,' she said, 'so don't worry if you're an anti-Semite. Actually, I take that back, not that I find Jews annoying, but that I don't worry about anti-Semites. They're worse than the Jews.'

'Boxers or briefs?' she said. 'Oh I hate it when guys wear briefs or boxer-briefs because it's like they're trapping their sweaty penis smell – sps – in. You pull down the waistband to suck a guy's cock and it's like a locker-room smell wafts toward your face. You gotta air that shit out. And protect your sperm. It's really the only thing attractive about you, like on a subliminal level. The potentiality of something better, beyond your disappointing existence. You know.'

'I know. And you're left feeling, what just happened? Who was that? How could this be? How can I go on? I must go on … I'm not so sure … Something's stopping … '

'My singing voice is stronger than ever, though … '

'If life, and like the formation of an ego, et cetera, like if life works on you like waves against a coastal shelf, like eroding you and forming you at the same time as you become an adult, then early heartbreak's like the tsunami in the formation of the adult ego-slash-coastal shelf. You know.'

'Yeah. Sure. It was fun. I'm glad you're a vegetarian.'

'I have to pee. I'm going to pee.'

'Yeah. And we always came together.'

'I hate dreams most of the time. I hate when the day's residue makes me dream of, like, me and Snooki doing surveillance for Michelle Obama. It's bullshit.'

'You've got a long way to go, buckaroo.'

'The Prophet's never accepted in her home country,' she said.

'Whatever. You're so gay, even if you think you're not. Three of your friends relentlessly hit on me and then you invite me in here with you. Don't think that has nothing to do with it.'

'The only good thing about dying is you really start to like life. What a joke.'

'Give an asshole a modicum of power ... I never want to subordinate anyone and I never want to be subordinated ... '

'I know it sounds cliché but he just fit. Everything, like not just his dick size. But he did get a bit of a *panza* and it did bother me, the way it rubbed up against me. I know that sounds superficial. It's weird.'

'I like Wodehouse because his novels are like antidepressants.'

'I don't want to be cremated. My life's ambition is to become a skeleton. At least for a little while.'

'She's about as empathetic as a boa constrictor.'

'People say *cellar door*'s the most like phonoaesthetically beautiful phrase but I prefer *lethal injection*.'

'We let film and video do far too much of our dreaming for us.'

'My theory on celebrity is that after twenty-one you're no longer a celebrity; it's democratizing.'

'Women are just so wildly beautiful that getting them pregnant, perhaps several times, altering their bodies, is the only way to get them to accept the monster that is Man. But I'm not saying women are so shit-hot in the end, either.'

'Sure – let me know.'

John Goldbach is the author of *The Devil and the Detective*, a novel, and *Selected Blackouts*, a story collection.

The author would like to thank the following:

T. F. Berger, T. Berry, J. Breakfast, T. Burke, A. Carless, S. Gordon, L. Henderson, K. Hutchinson, M. Iossel, P. E. Lessard, R. P. Lindsay, M. Maillet, M. Matthews, D. McGimpsey, J. Novakovich, J. Parker, V. Simmonds, M. Sutton, A. Sweetman, A. Szymanski, C. Tucker, H. Waechtler, B. Wainaina, E. Walsh and (esp.) A. Wilcox. And his friends and family, &c.

Typeset in Albertan. Albertan was designed by the late Jim Rimmer of New Westminster, B.C., in 1982. He drew and cut the type in metal at the 16pt size in roman only; it was intended for use only at his Pie Tree Press. He drew the italic in 1985, designing it with a narrow fit and a very slight incline, and created a digital version. The family was completed in 2005, when Rimmer redrew the bold weight and called it Albertan Black. The letterforms of this type family have an old-style character, with Rimmer's own calligraphic hand in evidence, especially in the italic.

Printed at the Coach House on bpNichol Lane in Toronto, Ontario, on Zephyr Antique Laid paper, which was manufactured, acid-free, in Saint-Jérôme, Quebec, from second-growth forests. This book was printed with vegetable-based ink on a 1965 Heidelberg KORD offset litho press. Its pages were folded on a Baumfolder, gathered by hand, bound on a Sulby Auto-Minabinda and trimmed on a Polar single-knife cutter.

Edited and designed by Alana Wilcox
Cover by Chris Tucker

Coach House Books
80 bpNichol Lane
Toronto ON M5S 3J4
Canada

416 979 2217
800 367 6360

mail@chbooks.com
www.chbooks.com